"You're hoping to adopt her?"

"I'm planning on it," Fern said with satisfaction. "As long as the birth father doesn't show up, I'm golden."

He cocked his head to one side. "You don't want her father to find her?"

"It's not like that. He's shown no interest in her for four years, so it's hardly likely he'll show up now. But we had to publish announcements for a few weeks to make sure he doesn't want her."

Carlo's head spun at her casual dismissal. He wanted to argue that just because a dad wasn't around, that didn't mean he was a deadbeat. Some dads didn't even know they had a child. But there was no need to argue with the woman who'd treated a stranger so kindly. "Mercy's kind of an old-fashioned name," he said instead.

She smiled. "Oh, that's just what I call her sometimes. Her mom did, too. Her full name is actually Mercedes."

The word slammed into his aching head with the force of a sledgehammer's blow. He had, indeed, blundered into the home of his own child.

Lee Tobin McClain read *Gone with the Wind* in the third grade and has been a hopeless romantic ever since. When she's not writing angst-filled love stories with happy endings, she's getting inspiration from her church singles group, her gymnastics-obsessed teenage daughter and her rescue dog and cat. In her day job, Lee gets to encourage aspiring romance writers in Seton Hill University's low-residency MFA program. Visit her at leetobinmcclain.com.

Books by Lee Tobin McClain

Love Inspired

Rescue River

Engaged to the Single Mom
His Secret Child

His Secret Child

Lee Tobin McClain

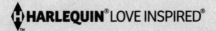

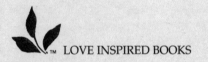 LOVE INSPIRED BOOKS

Recycling programs
for this product may
not exist in your area.

ISBN-13: 978-0-373-81893-8

His Secret Child

Copyright © 2016 by Lee Tobin McClain

www.Harlequin.com

Printed in U.S.A.

Then He said to them, "Whoever welcomes this little child in My name welcomes Me; and whoever welcomes Me welcomes the one who sent Me. For it is the one who is least among you all who is the greatest."
—*Luke* 9:48

For my daughter, Grace

Chapter One

Fern Easton looked at the fire she'd just built, then out the window at the driving snow, dim in the late-afternoon light. She shivered, but not because she was cold.

No, she was happy.

Two whole weeks to herself. Two whole weeks to work on her children's book in blessed peace.

As soon as she'd gotten home from the library, she'd shucked her sensible slacks and professional shirt and let her hair out of its usual tidy bun. Threw on her softest jeans and a comfortable fleece top. Next, she'd set up her drawing table in the living room of her friends' house.

House-sitting was awesome, because out here on the farm, no one would bother her.

Out here, she had a chance to fulfill her dream.

From the back room, her four-year-old daughter crowed with laughter over the antics of the animated mice and squirrels on the TV screen. Her *daughter*. Some days, Fern couldn't believe her good fortune.

She'd fed Bull, the ancient, three-legged bulldog she was babysitting as a part of the house-sitting deal. Puttering around like this, feeding an animal, taking care of her sweet child, was what she wanted, and determination rose in her to make it happen full-time.

She'd create a fantasy world with her books, and in her life, too. She wouldn't have to deal with the public or trust people who'd inevitably let her down. She wouldn't have to come out of her shell, listen to people telling her to smile and speak up. She wasn't really shy, she was just quiet, because there was a whole world in her head that needed attention and expression. And now, for two weeks, she got to live in that world, with a wonderful little girl and a loving old dog to keep her company.

She practically rubbed her hands together with glee as she poured herself a cup of herbal tea and headed toward her paints.

Knock, knock, knock.

She jerked at the unexpected sound, and worry flashed through her.

"Hey, Angie, I know you're in there!"

Fern felt her nose wrinkle with distaste. Some friend of the homeowners. Some male friend. Should she answer it?

More knocking, another shout.

Yeah, she had to answer. Anyone who'd driven all the way out here in a snowstorm deserved at least a polite word from her before she sent them away.

She opened the door to a giant.

He wore a heavy jacket and cargo pants. His face was made of hard lines and planes, only partly masked by heavy stubble. Intense, unsmiling, bloodshot eyes stared her down. "Who are you?"

Whoa! She took a step backward and was about to slam the door in this unkempt muscleman's face—she had her daughter's safety to think about, as well as her own—when Bull, the dog, launched his barrel-shaped body at the door, barking joyously, his stub of a tail wagging.

"Hey, old guy, you're getting around pretty good!" The man opened the door, leaned down.

"Hey!" Fern stepped back, then put her hands on her hips. "You can't come in here!"

The guy didn't listen; he was squatting down just inside the door to pet the thrilled bulldog.

Fern's heart pounded as she realized just how isolated she was. Never taking her eyes off him, she backed over to her phone and turned it on.

"Where's Troy and Angelica?" The man looked up at her. "And who're you?" His voice was raspy. Dark lines under his eyes.

"Who are *you*?"

He cocked his head to one side, frowning. "I'm Carlo. Angie's brother?"

Her jaw about dropped, because she'd heard the stories. "You're the missionary soldier guy!" She set her phone back down. "Really? What are you doing here?"

His eyes grew hooded. "Got some business to conduct here in the States. And I'm sick."

"Oh." She studied him. Maybe illness was the reason for his disheveled look.

"Your turn. Who are you? You supposed to be here?"

"My name's Fern. I'm house-sitting."

"Okay." He nodded and flashed an unexpected smile. "I didn't think you looked real dangerous."

The appeal of a smile on that rugged face left Fern momentarily speechless, warming her heart toward the big man.

"Thought I could bed down with my sister and get myself together before I get started with my…legal work. Where is she?"

"She's at Disneyland Paris." She said it reluctantly. "For two weeks."

"She's in Paris?" His face fell. "You've gotta be kidding."

She studied him. "Didn't you think to, like, call and check with her? When did you last talk?"

"It's been months. I don't...live a normal life. And like I said, I've been sick." He swayed slightly and unzipped his jacket. "Still have a little fever, but it's not catching."

"Hey. You don't look so good." In fact, he looked as though he was going to pass out, and then how would she ever get him out of here? She took his arm gingerly and guided him toward the couch. "You'd better sit down." She helped him out of his heavy, hooded, military-style jacket.

"I don't want to bother you..." He swayed again and sat down abruptly.

So now she had some giant guy who claimed to be Angelica's brother, smack dab in the middle of her living room. She studied him skeptically as she picked up her phone again. Dark gray sweater that didn't look any too new, heavy combat boots melting snow on the floor. Hmm.

Could he be acting this whole thing out in order to get in here and...what? Steal everything Troy and Angelica had? They were plenty comfortable, as evidenced by the Euro-Disney vacation, but they didn't put their money on display in expensive possessions, at least as far as she'd been able to tell in the few months she'd known Angelica.

What else could he want? Had someone told him she was going to be out here alone? She normally wasn't a skittish person, but this was different. This wasn't safe.

She was about to dial 911 when he said, "Let me call Ang. I have to figure out what to do next."

He reached in his pocket and pulled out an ancient-looking flip phone.

Fern walked to the back room to glance in on Mercedes. The child was fully immersed in her princess movie, a Friday-night treat Fern allowed reluctantly. For one thing, she wasn't overly fond of the princess phenomenon for little girls, and for another, she'd rather read Mercy storybooks than have her watch TV.

But those were preferences. Mercedes had watched princess movies with her mom, and it comforted her to watch them now.

Even one day with Mercedes was a blessing, but now she had the potential, even the likelihood, of adopting her permanently and for real. That was truly exciting. That was a dream much bigger than her dream of writing and illustrating children's books.

If she could create a nest for herself and a child—or six—who needed a home, and write on the side, she'd be the happiest woman on earth.

And maybe, just maybe, that was what God had in mind for her. Because she obviously wasn't suited to relating to other people, right? She wasn't cut out for marriage, nor couples entertaining, nor a singles life with a big close-knit group of friends.

But kids! Kids and books. And a dog or two, she thought, walking back out to the front room followed by the loyal Bull. She rubbed his graying head and let him give her a sloppy kiss. This was the life.

Or it would be, once she got rid of her un-invited guest.

"Stupid phone." Carlo shook his head and stared at the shiny black object in his hand. "It's not doing anything. I can't reach her."

"We can try my phone," Fern offered. She picked hers up and clicked through her few contacts, watching as the man removed his boots and set them on a newspaper beside the couch. Despite his size, he seemed very weak. Fern wasn't as afraid as she'd been before.

She put in the call. Felt a little bad about it—

she couldn't remember exactly what time it was in Paris, and she hated to wake up her friends.

No answer.

"Did you get a connection?" Carlo asked.

She shook her head. "Angelica bought some special plan to be able to talk over there. I should be able to get hold of her, but it might take a while."

The guy, Carlo, stared down at his hands. "I guess I'll be on my way, then."

"Where will you go?" she blurted out against her own will.

"I'll figure it out."

"Do you have friends in town? You grew up here, right?"

He nodded slowly, putting a forefinger and thumb on his forehead and massaging, as though it hurt. "I did grow up here. Unfortunately, I wasn't the most upright kid. So a lot of people have a bad impression of me."

"That's too bad. I don't think it's a judgmental town these days—at least, I haven't felt it to be—but maybe it was different in the past."

Carlo shrugged. "We were a pretty offbeat family. My parents made some enemies and I just added to the number. It's not Rescue River's fault."

That made her almost like him, that he admitted his own culpability rather than blaming everyone else but himself. A disease so many people seemed to have these days.

"Do you…would you like something to drink?"

"Yes, thank you." His face had taken on a greenish cast. "My head hurts pretty bad."

"Of course. Tea and aspirin?"

"Tea sounds good. I've got medicine."

Fern hurried into the kitchen and turned on the gas under her kettle to bring it back to a boil. It was so rare for her to have someone over, she barely knew how to handle it. But Carlo looked as though he was about to pass out.

What was she going to do? She couldn't have him stay. Oh, the place was plenty big, but she couldn't house a giant man who seemed to take up all the air in a room. She couldn't deal with company full-time.

Being solitary, living in her own head, was what had saved her as a foster child, shuttled from house to house, never fitting in, never really wanted. It had become a habit and a way of life. Nowadays, she preferred being alone. She thought longingly of her paints, of the children's story she was working on.

The water boiled and she fumbled through the cupboards, finding a mug and tea bag. Carried it out to the living room.

"Do you like milk and sugar… Oh. No, you don't."

He'd fallen asleep.

He'd tipped over right there on the couch and was breathing heavily, regularly.

No! That wouldn't do. She didn't want a stranger sleeping on the couch. She had to get him out of here. "Hey," she said, nudging him with her knee as she set the tea down beside him.

He leaped to his feet and grabbed her instantly in a choke hold, pulling her against his chest.

"Aaah! Hey!" She screamed, which made Bull start barking.

Carlo dropped his arms immediately and sidestepped away from her, lifting his hands to shoulder level. "Sorry. Sorry."

She backed halfway across the room and eyed him accusingly. "What was that for?"

"Jungle instinct," he said. "Sorry. I…don't do well when I'm startled. Did I hurt you?"

She rubbed her neck and stretched it from side to side as her heartbeat slowed back down to normal. "I'm fine." The truth be told, his closeness had had a very weird effect on her. She didn't like being grabbed, of course, but being forced to lean against that broad chest had given her a strange feeling of being…protected. Of being safe.

Which was ridiculous, because obviously, having him here was putting her and Mercedes at risk, not keeping her safe.

"Mama Fern? You okay?" The little-girl voice behind her was wary.

She turned, squatted down and smiled reassuringly. "Yeah, honey, I'm fine. C'mere." She held out her arms, and the little girl ran into them, nuzzling against her.

"I didn't know you had a child here." Carlo stood as if to come over toward them, and then swayed.

Fern wrapped her arms tighter around Mercedes. "Sit down and drink your tea," she ordered, gesturing toward it on the end table. "You look terrible. Do you know what's wrong? Have you seen a doctor?" She sat cross-legged and settled Mercedes in her lap.

"You ever hear of dengue fever?"

"Dengue! You have it?" The mother in her was glad it was indeed noncontagious.

He nodded. "You know what it is?"

"I'm a reference librarian, so I learn about all kinds of things like that. Do you have a bad case?"

"I hope not." He was rubbing the back of his neck again, as if it hurt. "It's been a couple of weeks and I thought I was better, but I'm weak. And apparently, it's possible to relapse, and if you do, it's pretty serious."

"Fatal sometimes."

"Thanks for reminding me."

"Sorry. Sit down."

He did, and drank the tea, and she watched him and stroked Mercy's hair and wondered how on earth she could get rid of him.

Carlo stared at the blurry woman and child across the room and wondered what to do.

His head was pounding and the pain behind his eyes was getting worse.

He reached out and brought the teacup to his lips, trying hard to hold it steady. Forced himself to drink. Staying hydrated was key.

"So you don't know anyone in town you could stay with?" she asked skeptically. "From growing up here, I mean?"

Well, let's see. He could stay with the family he'd bummed off when his parents had been too drunk or stoned to unlock the trailer door. Or maybe the teacher he'd lifted money from when his little sister had needed medicine they couldn't afford.

Or, who knew? Maybe some of the guys with whom he'd chugged six-packs in the woods had made good and would take him in.

Trouble was, he'd lost touch during his years in the jungle.

"I'm not sure. I can work something out. Stay with my grandfather, maybe." Although Angelica had said something about new rules at the Senior Towers, maybe they'd make an exception for an ailing veteran, if he and Gramps could resolve their differences long enough for him to ask nicely.

He tried to stand and the world spun.

"Sit down!" She sounded alarmed.

He did, wishing for a cold cloth to cover his eyes.

"Let me call the emergency room in Mansfield. You need a doctor."

He waved a hand. "Not really. All they can do is tell me to rest and wait it out."

"Oh." She bit at her lower lip. Whoever she was, she was real pretty. Long brown hair and fine bones and big eyes behind those glasses. The kind of woman he'd like to sit down and have a conversation with, sometime when he wasn't delirious. "Well," she continued, "do you think some food would make you feel better? Chicken soup?"

Something hot and salty sounded delicious. He'd slept through the meals on the plane and hadn't stopped for food on the drive from the airport. Maybe that was why he felt so low. "Yeah, food would be great."

"Be right back. C'mon, Mercy."

"Is he staying all night, Mama Fern?" The little girl didn't sound worried about it.

Somehow this Fern didn't strike him as the type who'd have men overnight casually. She looked way too guarded and buttoned up. But her little girl seemed perfectly comfortable with the notion of a man spending the night.

"No, he's not staying. But we're going to fix him a snack before he goes. Come on, you can help."

"Yay!" The little girl followed her mother and Carlo watched them go, feeling bemused.

How old was this little girl—maybe three or four?

Not far off from his own daughter's age, so he ought to pay attention, see what she did, what she liked. He needed to make a good first impression on the child he was coming to raise.

More than that, for now, he needed to figure out what to do. It was a blow that his sister wasn't here, and of course he should have called, had tried to call, but when he hadn't reached them, he'd figured she and her new husband would be here. They were newlyweds, practically, though Angelica's last note had let him know she was expecting a baby. And they also had a kid who was in full recovery from leukemia, his beloved nephew, Xavier. Not to mention that they ran a dog rescue. Shouldn't they be staying close to home?

It wasn't the first time he'd miscalculated. He seemed to be doing that a lot lately. So he'd eat whatever this pretty lady brought him, drink a lot of water. He'd hold off on those pain pills the doctor had given him, the ones with the mild narcotic, until he'd bedded down for the night. After his years in South and Central America, Carlo wasn't a fan of drugs in any form, and the last thing he needed was to feel any foggier. He needed to get himself strong enough to leave and find a place to stay. Tomorrow he'd talk to the lawyers and to his daughter's social worker and soon, very soon, he'd have his daughter. And he could start making amends for not trying hard enough to make his marriage work and for not considering that Kath could've been pregnant when she kicked him out that last time.

The woman—what had she said her name was? Fern?—came back out carrying a crockery bowl. She set it on a tray beside him, and the smell of soup tickled his nose, made him hungry for the first time in days. Behind her, the little girl carefully carried a plastic plate with a couple of buttered rolls on it.

It all looked delicious.

"I'll eat up and then be on my way," he promised, tasting the soup. *Wow. Perfect.* "This is fantastic," he said as he scooped another spoonful.

"Mama Fern always has good food."

Something about the way the little girl talked about her mother was off, but Carlo was too ecstatic about the chicken soup to figure out what it was.

"So…" The woman, Fern, perched on the other edge of the couch, watching him eat. "What are you going to do?"

He swallowed another spoonful. "As soon as I finish this soup—which is amazing—I'm going to head into Rescue River and see if I can find a place to stay."

"There's that little motel right on the edge of town. It tends to fill up during storms, though. Travelers coming through don't have a lot of choices."

"There's a few doors I can knock on." Not really, but she didn't need to know that. He could sleep in his truck. He'd slept in worse places.

Although usually, the problem was being too hot, not too cold. He'd have to find an all-night store and buy a couple of blankets.

"So what brought you out of the jungle?"

He paused in the act of lifting a spoon to his

mouth. She was being nosy and he hated that. But on the other hand, she was providing him with soup and bread and a place to sit down.

"You're nicer than my mommy's boyfriends." The little girl leaned on the couch and stared up at him.

He couldn't help raising an eyebrow at Fern.

Fern's cheeks turned a pretty shade of pink. "She's not talking about me. I'm kind of her foster mom."

"And she's gonna 'dopt me!"

"After all the grown-up stuff gets done, sweets."

They went on talking while Carlo slowly put down his spoon into his almost empty bowl of soup and stared at the two of them.

It couldn't be.

Could it?

It had to be a coincidence. Except, how many four-year-old girls were in need of being adopted in Rescue River, Ohio?

Could Fern have changed her name from Mercedes to Mercy?

No, not likely, but he'd learned during battle to consider all possibilities, however remote.

He rubbed his hand over his suddenly feverish face and tried to think. If this girl, by some weird set of circumstances, was Mercedes—his own kid, whom he hadn't known about until two weeks ago—then he needed to get out of here right away. He was making a terrible impression on someone who'd be sure to report every detail to the social workers.

Not only that, but his lawyer friend had advised him not to contact the child himself.

The child. Surely she wasn't his? The hair color was his own, but light brown hair was common. He studied her, amazed at her beauty, her curls hanging down her back, at her round, dark eyes. She was gorgeous. And obviously smart.

And obviously close with this woman who wanted to adopt her.

If this was foster care, then it was different from anything he'd imagined. He'd expected to find his daughter staying in a dirty old house filled to the brim with kids. No doubt that stereotype was from his own single bad experience years ago, but it was the reason he'd dropped everything, not waited to recover from his illness, and hopped a plane as soon as he realized he was a father and that his child's mother was dead.

He didn't want a child of his to suffer in foster care. He wanted to take care of her. And he would, because surely this beautiful child in this idyllic life was no relation to him.

When he did find his own daughter, he'd

find a way to make up for some of the mistakes of his past.

Maybe redeem himself.

"Are you finished?"

The pair had stopped talking and were staring at him. Oh, great. He was breathing hard and sweating, probably pale as paper.

"I'm done," he said, handing her the plate and bowl. "Thank you."

She carried them into the kitchen and he took the opportunity to study the child.

"How do you like it here?" he asked her.

"I like Bull," she said, "but home is nicer."

"Home with Mommy Fern?"

"Mama Fern. Yes."

"I guess you miss your mommy."

She looked at him. "Do you know her?"

He settled for "I don't think so." Because almost certainly, this wasn't his own child, whose mother, Kath, he had indeed known quite well. Theirs had been a mistaken marriage, born of lust and bad judgment. Soon after the wedding, they'd started having serious problems. Her drinking and drugs and promiscuous behavior had led to them breaking up, not once, but twice.

What he hadn't known was that the last time she'd kicked him out, he'd left her pregnant.

Fern walked back into the room and squatted down beside the child with a natural grace. "Half an hour till your bedtime, sweets. Want to have your snack in front of the TV? Finish your movie?"

"Yeah." The little girl hugged Fern. "Thanks for letting me."

"Fridays only. Let's get you set up."

Carlo's head was spinning so badly with questions and fever that he had to stay seated, but he forced himself to keep his eyes open and take deep breaths. Not only was he sick, but he was dizzy with confusion.

Could God have arranged it that he'd meet his child this way, rather than wearing nice clothes in a social worker's office?

Was that beautiful little girl his daughter?

Fern came back in. "She loves her princess movies," she said apologetically. "I'm not real big on TV for little kids, but it comforts her."

Carlo lifted his hands. "I'm not judging. Don't most kids watch TV?"

"Yeah, but…I want to do better."

She was a good, caring foster mom. And he had to find out the truth. "How old did you say she is?"

"She's four, going on five."

He nodded. "Now, did you name her Mercy or was that already her name?"

She looked at him as if he had lost his mind.

"You can't change a four-year-old's name. She's been Mercy all her life."

Relief poured over him. He hadn't messed up the all-important moment of meeting his own daughter. To be polite, he tried to keep the conversation going. "And you're…hoping to adopt her?"

"I'm planning on it," she said with satisfaction. "Everything's looking great. As long as the birth father doesn't show up, I'm golden."

He cocked his head to one side. "You don't want her father to find her?"

She shook her head impatiently. "It's not like that. He's shown no interest in her for four years, so it's hardly likely he'll show up now. Typical deadbeat dad, but we had to publish announcements for a few weeks to make sure he doesn't want her."

Carlo's head spun at her casual dismissal. He wanted to argue that just because a dad wasn't around, that didn't mean he was a deadbeat. Some dads didn't even know they had a child. But there was no need to argue with the woman who'd treated a stranger so kindly. "Mercy's kind of an old-fashioned name," he said instead.

She smiled. "Oh, that's just what I call her sometimes. Her mom did, too. Her full name is actually Mercedes."

The name slammed into his aching head with the force of a sledgehammer's blow. He had indeed blundered into the home of his own child.

Chapter Two

Fern frowned at the man on her couch. He was pale, his forehead covered in a fine sheen of sweat. Great, just great. The poor man was deathly ill.

Maybe he should go to the hospital. Didn't the ER have to take everyone, regardless of their ability to pay? Although the nearest ER was quite a ways off...

She walked over to the window, flipped on an outdoor light and gasped. Huge snowflakes fell so thickly that it was hard to see anything, but she could make out thigh-high drifts next to the porch.

"What's wrong?" She heard his slow footsteps as he came over to stand behind her.

His looming presence made her uncomfortable. "It's getting worse out there."

"I should go." He turned, swayed and grabbed

the back of a chair with one hand and her shoulder with another. "Whoa. Sorry."

Compassion warred with worry in her heart. "Why don't you at least take a little nap? You're not looking so good."

"I… Maybe I will. Don't know if I can make it to my truck."

She helped him to the couch, even though having his arm draped over her shoulder felt strange. The few guys she'd dated had been closer to her own small size, not like this hulking giant, and they tended not to snuggle up. Something about her demeanor didn't invite that.

She helped him down onto the couch and noticed he was shivering. Finding a quilt, she brought it over and spread it out across his body. Located a more comfortable pillow and helped him lift his head to slide it underneath.

His hair felt soft, and he smelled clean, like soap.

"Thanks, I really appreciate…this." His blue eyes drifted shut.

Fern watched him for a few minutes to make sure he was really out. Then she watched the end of the princess movie cuddling with Mercedes, and then carried her up to bed on her back, cautioning her to be quiet because of the man sleeping in the living room.

"Who is he, Mama Fern?"

"He's our friend Angelica's brother. You know Xavier? This man is his uncle."

"I like Xavier," Mercedes said with a little hero worship in her voice. "He's in first grade."

"That's right."

Fern read two picture books and then, firmly denying the request for a third, turned off the light.

She grabbed a novel and sat down on the floor outside the child's bedroom.

Sometimes nights were hard for Mercedes. She still missed her mom.

But tonight was a good night. Within minutes, Mercedes had drifted off and was breathing the heavy, steady breath of a child in sleep.

Fern went back downstairs quietly, picked up her phone and headed to the kitchen where her sleeping housemates couldn't hear her.

This time, the call went through and a couple of minutes later, she was talking to her yawning friend Angelica. "What? Carlo's there?"

"He's asleep on the couch even as we speak."

"Let me go out in the hall so I don't wake my boys. I can't believe this!" Angelica's voice proved that she'd come wide-awake. "I haven't seen him for a couple of years, except for a few minutes at our wedding. Why'd he have to show up now, instead of last week?"

"He didn't even stay for the whole wedding?"

"No, he stayed. And at our house after for a night, but I was with my husband." Her voice went rich and happy.

Sudden hot jealousy flashed through Fern. Why couldn't *she* ever feel that joy that seemed to come so readily to other fortunate women?

She got a grip on herself. What was wrong with her? She was truly happy for her friend. She explained about Carlo's fever. "He's pretty sick, and he said that's why he hadn't called first. I just wanted to touch base with you because…well, he's a stranger and I don't know if it's safe to have him here. I mean, I know you and I'd trust you with my life, and Mercedes's, but…"

"I totally understand." Angelica paused, obviously thinking. "I wonder who he could stay with. We could call Troy's brother, Sam, and see if he could stay out there. Or Gramps. He could bunk down at the Senior Towers. They have a new rule about no guests staying overnight, but maybe they'll bend it for Carlo, at least for one night." She sounded doubtful.

"I hate to make him go," Fern said. "It's snowing something awful."

"Carlo's been in much worse places. He's very tough. He can handle a little drive in the snow."

"I don't know. He's pretty shaky."

"Let me make a few calls," Angelica said with a huge yawn. "I'm sure I can get hold of somebody who'll take him in, if this phone doesn't glitch again."

"It's okay, you go back to sleep. I can call Sam or your grandpa." Fern's shy side cringed at the notion of talking to men she barely knew, but it would be worth it to get the disconcerting Carlo out of her house.

"Oh, could you? That would be so wonderful. We had a long day, and Xavier didn't want to go to sleep, and…"

"And you're frazzled. Go back to bed. I'll deal with Carlo."

"Thanks so much! And, Fern, he's a totally trustworthy guy, okay? A real hero. He took incredible care of me when I was a kid. He managed everything when our parents couldn't, and got Gramps to take me in. Plus, he's done all kinds of top-secret military stuff. Has a security clearance that's a mile high. And he's served as a missionary in all kinds of super-dangerous places. So you're safe with him, whatever happens."

They said their goodbyes and Fern stared at the man on the couch. A military hero, huh? And a missionary to boot.

But as she studied him, another thought

crossed her mind: What if he wasn't Carlo? What if he was a criminal who'd just assumed that name and identity? Sure, Bull had acted friendly, but maybe the guy had a pocket full of good-smelling dog treats.

How could she verify that this guy on her couch was in fact Carlo, Angelica's brother, the war hero?

She walked around the house, looking at the photo groupings, but she didn't see any that included Angelica's brother. Of course, he hadn't been around lately, but you'd think she would have old pictures of him…

Except that the two of them had grown up in chaos, and Angelica had struggled, really, right up until she'd reconnected with Troy. So there were no pictures of Xavier and his uncle Carlo; Angelica probably hadn't even had a phone.

She saw a khaki-colored duffel bag by the door, next to his jacket, and an idea crossed her mind.

She looked back at the stranger, watching the steady rise and fall of his chest.

Then she walked over toward his things. Surely he'd have identification there, or at least something to verify his identity. To put her mind at ease. Searching the man's belongings wasn't the most ethical thing to do, but she had a child to protect.

And if she was going to search, she needed to do it now, while he slept.

A quick check of his jacket pockets revealed nothing, so she undid the knots that tied the duffel shut, moving slowly and carefully. Given how he'd jumped up and grabbed her, he was obviously pretty sensitive to noise. She had to be utterly silent.

She eased the bag open and then tensed as his breathing changed. He shifted over to his side while she sat, frozen, watching him.

As soon as he breathed steadily again, she parted the edges of the bag.

The first thing she saw was an eight-inch hunting-type knife, in an old-looking leather case that would go on a belt.

Well, okay, then. He hadn't taken *that* through airport security, no way.

She picked it up with the tips of two fingers, pulled it out of the duffel, and set it beside her on the floor.

Digging on through, she found some trail mix, a thriller paperback and a Bible that had seen hard use. She took the risk of flipping through it and saw underlining, highlighting, turned-down pages.

Wow. He took his faith seriously. What would that be like? Since being saved, Fern attended church most Sundays and read a devotional book every night before she went to sleep, but she'd never gone so far as to study the Bible on her own.

He certainly didn't fit the stereotype of a Bible scholar, but Angelica had said he was a missionary. And anyway, who was she to judge? The fact that he had books, especially a Bible, was a point in his favor. Not quite enough to counteract that deadly looking knife, though.

Next, she found a vest. Camo colored, made of heavy nylon, with pouches that held hard plates. She pulled it out a little, making a slight clatter, and her heart pounded as she went still, turning her gaze to the man on the couch.

He shifted but didn't open his eyes.

Whew. He was really out. She studied the vest more closely. A bulletproof, military-style vest? But why?

She put the vest down, thinking through the few facts she knew about Angelica's brother. He'd been a good uncle to Xavier, a male influence who'd gotten him into sports when he was little. He'd been in the military, and right before Xavier became sick, Carlo had gotten the call to the missionary field. Come to think of it, she didn't know whether the call was from a person or from God. Why hadn't she listened more closely?

And if he'd gone into the missionary field more than two years ago, why were a bullet-proof vest and hunting knife in the top of his overnight bag?

She rummaged underneath the vest and pulled out a photo in a metal frame, of Carlo squatting down in the midst of a group of ragged, dark-skinned boys. In the background was jungle-type vegetation and a leaf-covered hut. All of them, Carlo and the boys, were smiling broadly. The younger ones were pressed close to Carlo and he had his arms around them.

So he liked kids. Reassuring.

She wasn't finding the ID she wanted, but she was finding evidence of a man with a complicated life.

She fumbled further and found a piece of notebook paper, folded over twice and much crumpled. She opened it up.

"Dear Uncle Carlo, I miss yu pls come hom."

The signature was a scrawled XAVIER.

Fern drew in a deep breath and let it out, some of her fears abating.

She hadn't found an ID, but she believed in the man now. He was Angelica's brother, and if his possessions were any indication, he cared about kids, especially his nephew. Why else would he keep the letter from Xavier?

Carefully, she replaced all the items in the bag and closed it up. Then she sat back on her heels and studied the man.

He was breathing evenly, now lying on his side. He had short hair and his skin was bronzed, and there were creases at the corners of his eyes. Obviously a guy who spent most of his time outside.

She tried to remember what Angelica had told her about him. Their friendship had started at church, so it wasn't that old. It was natural that Angelica had talked about her brother's missionary work, but hadn't she also mentioned something about a marriage that hadn't worked out, somewhere out West? If she remembered right, Angelica hadn't even had the chance to meet Carlo's wife—the marriage had been too brief and chaotic.

His arms bulged out the edges of the T-shirt he was wearing, but his face had relaxed in sleep, erasing most of the harshness.

Here was a soldier, but also a missionary. With a well-worn Bible. Who cared about kids.

As she watched him, she was aware of a soft feeling inside that she rarely felt. Aware that her heart was beating a little bit faster.

How ridiculous. He was nothing like the few

guys she'd gone out with before—mostly pale, video-gaming types. If he'd ever set foot in the children's room of a library, she'd be surprised.

And there was no way he'd look at the likes of her! She only attracted supernerds. She was a boring librarian who never left Ohio. She couldn't keep up with him.

"Quit staring."

"What?" She jumped about six feet in the air.

"Did you like what you found?" he asked lazily.

"What I... What do you mean?" Fern felt her face flashing hot.

"In my bag."

"You were awake!" She felt totally embarrassed because of her thoughts, because of how long she'd sat staring at him. Had he been watching her, too? What had he been thinking?

"I'm a trained soldier. I wake up when you blink. So don't try to pull one over on me." He was half smiling, but there was wariness in his eyes. "What were you looking for?"

"Um, an ID? I wanted to see if you were really Angelica's brother. I talked to her, but then I thought you might not be Carlo at all."

"You didn't find an ID in there," he said flatly, "so why aren't you calling the police?"

"Or pulling your own nasty-looking knife on you? Because of your letter from Xavier."

"What?"

"You had a letter from Xavier. And it was folded and refolded, almost to where it's tearing at the creases. So that means you looked at it a bunch of times. You really care about your nephew, don't you?"

A flush crept up his cheeks. "Yeah. He's a good kid."

"And maybe you're not a terrible guy. Or at least, maybe you're who you say you are." Awkward, awkward. Fern was way too awkward with people, especially men. Being alone was way more comfortable and safe.

Carlo tried to sit up, pulling on the back of the couch to shift his weight to a sitting position. The room only spun for a minute.

He had to get out of here before his pretty hostess dug deeper into his stuff or his psyche and found out something he didn't want known.

Bad enough that she'd found a hunting knife in his bag. He checked his ankle holster reflexively, even though he knew his weapon was safe there.

Her phone buzzed and she checked the front of it. Worry creased her face as she punched a message back. Then she got up and turned on the TV.

The weather analysts were in their glory as she flipped from station to station.

"It's being called the storm of the century!"

"If you don't have to go out, don't go out!"

"Stay tuned for a list of closings!"

Finally, she settled on the local station he remembered from his childhood. A reporter stood in front of an overturned tractor trailer on the interstate as snow blew his lacquered hair out of control. "Folks, it looks as if things are only going to get worse for the next couple of days. All nonemergency vehicles are advised to stay off the roads, and several of our rural counties have just issued complete road closings…"

Great. He needed to get out while he could. He stood to go and her phone buzzed again. She answered and as he chugged the rest of his tea and reached for his boots, he heard one side of an intense conversation that seemed to be about dogs.

When she clicked off the phone, she looked worried.

"What's going on?" he asked. "I mean, besides the snowstorm. I need to get out of here while I can."

"They've actually closed the roads between

here and town," she said. "And the people Troy and Angelica hired to take care of the dogs can't get out here."

"How many dogs?"

"Something like forty."

"That's a lot. Where?"

She walked to the window that faced the back of the house and gestured out. When he put his face to the glass and looked, he saw the vague outline of a barn about a football field's distance away. It came back to him then, from Angie's wedding: the size of the barn, the number of dogs Troy and Angelica housed inside.

When he walked to the other window and looked out toward his truck, it was completely obscured. As was that path that had led to it.

He rubbed the back of his neck, thinking. He really, really wanted to get out of here, and he was sure he could make it in his truck.

On the other hand, he hated to leave a woman and child alone out here. "How are you going to take care of the dogs?"

"I'll get it done." She straightened her shoulders as worry creased her forehead. "How hard can it be?"

"Pretty hard. You've never done it before?"

"No, but one of their usual helpers can coach me through it by phone."

He studied the storm, then turned back to

look at the petite woman in front of him. Taking care of forty dogs meant a lot of messy kennels to clean. There'd be heavy bags of food to carry, water to fetch, medications to dispense if any of them were sick. And from what his sister had told him, they weren't the easiest dogs.

He made a snap decision. "I'd better stay and help you." Even as he said it, his heart sank. That was the last thing he wanted to do.

"Excuse me? I'll be the one issuing invitations. Which I didn't do."

"Sorry to be rude. But there's no way you can manage all those dogs alone. What will you do with your daughter?"

"I don't know, but I'll figure it out, okay? Look, I don't even know you."

He nodded. "I know. It's not exactly comfortable, is it? I can sleep in my truck or in the barn."

She tossed her head back, looking at the sky. "There's no way that will work! The barn and the bunkhouse aren't winterized, not well enough for a person to stay, and you'll freeze to death in your truck. And you're sick!" She bit her lip and looked around, struggle evident on her face.

"I assume you'll give me a blanket if I'm extranice?" He meant to lighten her mood, but the line came out sounding flirtatious. *Great move, Camden.*

She ignored him. "I guess," she said slowly, "you can stay in the TV room. And I'll lock the doors upstairs."

"If you're sure, that would be fantastic." It was a shame that women had to be so careful, but they did. And he was glad his daughter—his *daughter*, he could still barely wrap his mind around that concept—was safe with someone like stern, protective, beautiful Fern.

She was worrying her lower lip. "For now, I'd better check on Mercy and then go out and make sure the dogs are okay. They got their dinner, but I want to make sure they're warm enough. Let them out into their runs one last time."

"I'll go with you." He stood and got his feet under him.

"No! You don't need to come." Then she bit her lip, and he couldn't help thinking how cute she was. Not a stereotypical librarian at all, despite the thick glasses.

"What?"

"I…I guess I don't want you to stay here alone with Mercy, either."

"Then, you'll have to accept my help. As much as I can do anyway. Bull can watch over…your little girl." Whoa, he had to be careful what he said until he decided how he was going to punt.

She let out a sigh and he recognized it. "Not a people person, eh? Me, either. We don't have to talk."

She stared at him. "You get that?"

"I get that. I've got an introverted side myself."

She raised an eyebrow and then put on her coat and sat down to pull furry boots over her skinny jeans. "I guess I could use some help, come to think of it. It's like a *Little House on the Prairie* storm. Wonder if we should tie a line from the house to the barn."

"Not a bad idea," he said. "But I think we'll be able to see our way back. The structures are bigger than in Laura Ingalls Wilder's day."

She stared at him again. "Why do you know about Laura Ingalls Wilder?"

"Because I have a little sister," he said. "I used to get books at the library for her all the time. Those were some of her favorites. Mine, too, if you want to know the truth."

"You're a sensitive soldier?"

"More like a desperate big brother." He chuckled. "It was either books or playing with her one and only Barbie doll. I couldn't stomach that."

She opened the door and cold wind cut into

Carlo's body like a frigid knife. He wasn't used to this, not after years in the tropics. "You ready?" he asked, shrugging into his jacket.

"I guess. But if you collapse out there, I don't think I can drag you back."

"I won't collapse." In truth, he felt better after the meal and the bit of a nap. Strong enough to make it out to the barn, which he could barely see through the whiteout conditions. Maybe a rope wasn't a bad idea, at that.

He broke a path all the way to where the dogs were, checking back frequently to make sure she still followed. She was small boned and thin, and the cold and wind had to affect her more than it did him, but she pushed on without complaining.

When they got to the kennels, she took the lead, unlocking the gate and then the barn door, letting herself in to a chorus of barking. She approached each dog, touching them, clucking at them, and they calmed down quickly.

Okay, so on top of being cute and maternal, she was a dog whisperer.

And she was raising his daughter and hoping to keep the child away from her worthless birth father, he reminded himself. She was his enemy, not his friend. He was here to learn more about her, not admire her looks or skills.

"If you start at that end, we can let out whoever wants out," she said, nodding toward the kennels closest to the door.

He knew from his sister's notes that most of the dogs were bully breeds because Troy, who owned the rescue, took in dogs that wouldn't otherwise find a home. As he started opening kennels, he could see that some were scarred, probably from abuse or neglect. But their rough background didn't mean they were stupid; most elected not to go out in the storm. When he finished his side, he checked the heating unit.

Fern was taking twice as long as he was to work with the dogs, and he realized she was patting and playing a little with each one. She was obviously unafraid of them, even though several stood as tall as her waist.

Carlo started letting out the dogs on her side, this time taking a little more energy to pat and talk to them.

By the time they met in the middle, he was feeling feverish again, but he still needed to keep the energy to get back to the house. "Ready to go back?"

"Sure. You look done in."

"I am. But I'll do my best not to collapse on you." He tried to smile.

"At least let me lead this time."

"No, it's…"

But she was already out the door. She obviously was a woman who did what she wanted to do, who, despite appearing shy, was very independent. Okay, then. He could respect that.

The storm had grown even worse. His breath froze and the wind whipped his face, and despite the fact that he'd broken a path and had someone walking in front of him, Carlo came close to losing his footing several times. His head was swimming.

Then Fern stumbled and fell into a thigh-deep snowdrift.

He reached for her, braced himself and pulled her out, and as he steadied her, he felt a sudden stunning awareness of her as a woman.

She looked up into his eyes and drew in a sharp breath.

Did she feel what he felt, or was the closeness a distinct displeasure?

Wind squealed around the fence posts, and whiteness was all he could see. Whiteness and her face. "Come on," he said into her ear. "We've got to get inside."

She pulled away from him and soldiered on toward the house, tossing a mistrustful look over her shoulder.

It was going to be a long night.

Chapter Three

Fern woke up to silence, utter silence. The light in the room was amazing. She walked to the window and gazed out into a world of soft white mounds overlaid with a crystalline sparkle. Sunlight peeked through a gap in heavy clouds that suggested the snowstorm wasn't done with them yet.

When you see the wonder of God's creation, how can you doubt Him? She smiled as her friend Kath's words came back to her, even as she marveled at her friend's faith. Despite Kath's horrendous past and her illness, she'd been able to praise God and had taught Fern to do the same.

She slipped out of bed and went to her bedroom door.

Locked.

Oh, yeah. The stranger.

As if a locked door could stop a man of Carlo's skills. But it had made her rest a little easier.

Her feeling of peace shaken, she took a deep breath and headed down the hall into Mercedes's room. Maybe the stranger would sleep for a long time. He certainly needed to; by the end of the evening last night, he'd looked awful.

She frowned at the intrusion into her safe world. She'd wanted to be out here alone, not hosting a stranger. A disturbing stranger.

Why was he so disturbing?

Because you're attracted to him, an inner voice said.

She shook her head. She didn't want to be attracted to him. To anyone, really, but especially to this jock type who was so handsome, so far out of her league. She didn't need to get her heart broken. She needed to protect it, because she needed to stay sane for Mercedes. Opening herself up to feelings would make all the bad stuff come back in, and she just wasn't ready for that.

She opened Mercy's door and walked over to the child's bed. She was staying in Xavier's room, so the surroundings were pure boy: race-car sheets, soccer trophies, toy trains and a big container of LEGO blocks.

Even in that setting, Mercedes glowed with girliness in her pink nightgown, her long curls spread across the pillow.

Fern's heart caught inside her. She'd never loved anyone so much in her life. And if she could save one child, maybe more, from the pain she'd been put through as a ward of the state, she'd have done a lot.

Mercedes was sleeping hard. For better or worse, she was a late riser. Well, Fern would take advantage of the time and the light to do some artwork.

She grabbed a diet soda out of the refrigerator, not wanting to take the time to make coffee, and headed right toward her worktable. Sat down, got out her paints and immersed herself in capturing the snowy scene out the window.

A while later—minutes? Hours? She couldn't tell—she smelled something that plunged her straight back to her own childhood. The memory was mixed, and she painted awhile longer, taking advantage of her own heightened emotions to evoke more feelings with her art.

"Breakfast's ready!"

The deep voice startled her, making her smear a stroke of paint. She jumped up and turned around. The sight of Carlo with a spatula in hand disoriented her.

"Whoa," he said, approaching her with concern. "I didn't mean to scare you."

Fern pressed a hand to her chest. "It's fine. What's that smell?"

"Bacon. I hope it's okay…"

"You got in the fridge and took out bacon and cooked it?" Her voice rose to a squeak. "Really?"

"Yeah, well, I figured Angelica would have some. Actually, it was in the freezer. But I also stole some eggs, which may have been yours. And they're getting cold. Where's Mercedes?"

Fern was still trying to wrap her mind around the fact that this…this man was cooking in her kitchen. Well, her friend's kitchen, but still. She'd never had a man in her home. She didn't know how to handle it. Didn't want to know.

"Mama Fern?" Mercedes's plaintive voice from the top of the stairs gave Fern a welcome focus.

She hurried up and wrapped her arms around the child. "Hey there, sleepyhead. What's going on?"

"What's cooking? It smells yummy."

"Um…bacon." Up until this moment, Fern hadn't intended to eat any; she wanted to get this man out of the house quickly, not break bread with him.

But if Mercedes liked bacon, then bacon it would be. "Our guest cooked breakfast," she explained. "Let's wash your face and hands and you can come on down and eat."

Minutes later, the three of them sat around the wooden table. Carlo had served up plates of bacon, eggs and toast, and he'd even poured orange juice and set out fruit on the side.

"This is good," Mercedes said, her mouth full, jam on the side of her face.

"It sure is good, Mercy-Mercedes." He made a funny face at the little girl, and she burst out in a torrent of giggles.

Fern's breath caught.

Amazing that Mercedes could still be so happy and trusting, given the difficulties of life with her mother and then the loss of her. Amazing that she, Fern, got to raise this incredible child.

And it was amazing to be sitting here around the table with a child and a handsome, manly man who knew his way around the kitchen and could joke around with a child.

Thing was, Carlo was trouble.

Oh, he'd been questionable when he showed up here on her doorstep, sick and wild looking. But that man, that kind of trouble, she'd been able to handle.

Now, seeing him feeling better and being

charming and domestic, she felt the twin weights of longing and despair pressing down on her heart.

She wanted a family.

She'd always wanted a family, wanted it more than anything. She hadn't had one, even as a child.

But there was no way she could form a family with any man worth the having. She just wasn't the type. She was shy, and awkward, and unappealing. She wore thick glasses and read books all the time and didn't know how to flirt or giggle.

So the part of her that looked around the table and wished for something like this, forever, just needed to be tamped down.

She couldn't have it and she needed to stop wanting it.

Abruptly, she stood up. "I've got to go feed the dogs."

"But, Mama Fern, *I* want to come see the dogs."

Fern hesitated. The animals were generally good, but they were just so big and strong. The idea of having a four-year-old—her own precious four-year-old—in their vicinity was a little too scary.

Carlo put a hand on her arm and she jerked away at the burn of it, staring at him.

His eyebrows went up and he studied her. "Sorry."

"It's okay. I'm jumpy." Awkward, awkward.

"Let's finish breakfast, and then we can all go out together."

"Yeah!" Mercedes shouted.

Oh, great. More pseudo–family togetherness. "That's fine," Fern said. "I'm going to start the dishes."

"But you haven't finished your—"

"I'm not hungry," she interrupted, and it was true. Her appetite had departed the moment those feelings of inadequacy and awkwardness and unlovableness arose in her.

She carried her dishes to the counter, fuming. Why had he shown up? Why hadn't he left her there in peace, to do her art and create some kind of family, even if not the real or the best kind?

You couldn't have handled the dogs alone, a voice of logic inside her said. *Maybe God's looking out for you. Maybe He sent a helper.*

But did He have to send a helper who was so handsome, who woke those desires for something she could never have?

She scrubbed hard at the pan that had held

the bacon and eggs. Looked out the window toward the kennels, and breathed, and tried to stuff her feelings back down.

"What were you working on in there?" Carlo asked.

"What do you mean?" On the defensive.

"Your easel. Your art."

"I…I do some writing and illustrating."

"Really? Can I see?'

"No!" She grabbed a towel to dry her hands and hurried toward the easel, bent on covering her work.

Carlo scooted his chair back to watch her from the kitchen. "Hey, it's okay. I wouldn't have looked without your permission."

"I'm just… It's silly. I…I don't like to show anyone my work before it's done." Truth to tell, her stories and illustrations were the one place she felt safe to delve into her own issues, to the challenges of her past. Sometimes, she felt it was all too revealing, but she was so driven to do it.

She could do her children's books and raise a family just fine. But to have a handsome man looking through her stuff, making fun of it maybe, asking questions—that she couldn't deal with. No way.

The wall phone's ringing was a welcome respite. She tucked the cover over her easel and hurried over to it.

"Hello?"

"Fern, it's Lou Ann Miller. From church?"

Fern vaguely remembered a tart, smiling, gray-haired woman who often sat with Troy and Angelica. "Hi, Lou Ann."

"Listen, I had an email from Angelica waiting for me this morning, and she let me know you have some unexpected company. Are you all right? How's Mercy?"

"We're doing fine." Fern looked at Mercedes. Carlo had found a clean dishcloth, wetted it and was washing off the child's messy face and hands, making silly faces to keep her from fussing about it.

"That's great. And don't worry about your new helper. He has a good heart."

"You know him?" She heard her own voice squeak.

"Oh, yes. I've known that boy most of his life." Lou Ann chuckled. "Pretty rough around the edges, isn't he?"

Fern looked at the man who'd invaded her safe haven. Even playing with an innocent little child in front of the fire, he looked every inch a mercenary: thick stubble, bulging biceps, shadowy, watchful eyes. "Yes," she said, swallowing. "Yes, he is."

* * *

Carlo sat on the floor building a block tower with the child he was almost certain was his daughter. He studied her small hands, her messy curls, her sweet, round cheeks.

His daughter's foster mother was talking to someone named Lou Ann on the phone. Probably Lou Ann Miller, who had to be getting old these days. He remembered stealing pumpkins from her front porch with a big gang of his friends. She'd chased after them and called all of their parents.

All the other boys had gotten punished. Not him, though. His parents had thought it was funny.

As he'd grown up, he'd realized that their neglect wasn't a good thing, especially when he'd seen how it affected his younger sister. When he'd had to take up their slack. He'd judged his folks pretty harshly.

But they'd been there at least some of the time. Unlike him, for his own daughter. How had it never occurred to him that Kath could have gotten pregnant during their brief reconciliation?

He wanted to clasp Mercedes tight and make up for the previous four years of her life. He wished he could rewind time and see her first smile, her first step.

But no. He left his wife pregnant and alone, and even though she'd kicked him out without telling him the truth about the baby she carried, had pressured him into signing the divorce papers, he should have tried harder. A lot harder.

Kath's letter, which had apparently languished for a couple of months before reaching him, had just about broken his heart. She'd found the Lord, and moved to Rescue River because she'd liked the way he'd described it and wanted to raise their daughter there.

Apparently, she'd even thought there was a chance they could remarry and raise Mercedes together. Sometime later, after he'd sown his wild oats and come back home to the States.

But it had turned out they didn't have the time for that. Kath had found out she was dying, and that was when she'd written to him, telling him about Mercedes and urging him to come home and take care of his daughter. She'd kept his identity secret from her social worker in case he wasn't able to come home—warped Kath logic if he'd ever heard of it. So until the social worker received the copy of Kath's letter he'd mailed and verified the information, even she wouldn't know there was an interested, responsible father in the picture.

Which was how Mercedes had ended up with Fern, apparently.

Carlo ran his hand through his hair and almost groaned aloud. He shouldn't have given up on their marriage so readily, but the truth was, he'd realized there was no more love or connection between them. Kath had been deep into a partying lifestyle she hadn't wanted to change. Reuniting would have been such an uphill battle that he hadn't minded when she'd kicked him out after just a week.

He was no good at relationships, never had been. But he hated that he'd left her to struggle alone. And even more, he hated that he'd left this innocent child to be raised by an unstable mother.

So now he was going to try to fix what had gone wrong. Maybe he'd failed as a husband. He'd failed at getting Kath into rehab. Failed as a father, so far.

But now that he knew about her existence, he was determined not to fail Mercedes. No, sir, never again. Though he was horrible at intimate relationships, he got along okay with kids. Even had a gift for working with them, according to his friends in the missionary field. Ironic that he, the guy who scared off most women and a lot of men, seemed to connect effortlessly with kids.

When Fern got off the phone, he stuffed down his feelings and made his face and voice bland. The first step in getting his daughter back was to find out what had been going on in her life. "Everything okay?"

Fern nodded, biting her lip. That was a habit of hers, he noticed. And it was really distracting, because she had full, pretty lips.

"Who was that?"

She gave him a look that said he'd overstepped his boundaries.

"Miss Lou Ann, from church," Mercedes said. "She gave me a toothbrush. Want to see?"

"Sure," Carlo said, and watched the child run toward the stairs, his heart squeezing in his chest.

"Lou Ann Miller gives all the children toothbrushes. Musical ones. She doesn't believe in candy."

"That figures. I remember her."

Fern cocked her head to one side. "She remembers you, too."

"I don't doubt it." He studied Fern and risked a question. "How'd you end up taking care of Mercedes anyway?"

She hesitated.

Easy, easy. "No need to tell me if you don't want to. I'm just curious."

Fern perched on the hearth and started stacking blocks absently. "It's okay. I need to get used to talking about it. But it's a sad story."

Carlo's stomach twisted with shame. He was, at least in part, responsible for the sadness.

"She's my friend Kath's little girl. Kath wasn't in town that long, but she made a huge difference in my life. We got...super close. And then she died." Fern's voice cracked just as Mercedes came trotting back down the stairs, musical toothbrush in hand.

"Look, mister! It makes a song!" She shook it vigorously and then looked up and touched Fern's face. "Why you sad, Mama Fern?"

"Just thinking about your mama."

"Oh." Mercedes nodded. "Bye!" she said suddenly, and ran across the room to a pink case full of dolls and doll clothes.

Fern chuckled. "Kids. When they don't want to talk about something, you know it."

Carlo had to know. "What...what did she say about Mercedes's dad? Was he ever in the picture?"

"She didn't talk much about him. Said he had issues. But what kind of guy would leave a terminally ill woman to cope with their little daughter alone?"

That was the question.

He had a lot to make up for, and it started with helping his daughter right now, stranded in the storm.

Given how fiercely protective Fern seemed,

he didn't think he could explain his role in the situation without arousing her ire and getting kicked out. And then how would the pair cope, given that the snow was starting up again?

No, better to wait out the storm without revealing his identity. Once it was over, he could see about paternity tests and get advice from a lawyer about how to proceed.

Meanwhile, he could help out a vulnerable child and foster mom. Maybe start to absolve himself of some of his misdeeds. Get to know little Mercedes.

Redeem himself. If that was even possible.

Chapter Four

For Carlo the late-morning trip out to the kennels was completely different from the night before.

It was daylight, and snowing hard.

And he was carrying Mercedes.

Just the feel of those little arms curled trustingly around his neck as he fought his way through thigh-high snowdrifts made his heart swell. He wasn't worthy, he didn't deserve it, but God had given him this moment, a blessing to cherish.

"You doing okay, sweets?" came Fern's voice from behind him.

Was she calling *him* sweets?

"I'm fine, Mama Fern," Mercedes piped up, and Carlo realized his mistake. Oh, well, it had felt nice for that one second. He shook his head and kept moving steadily toward the barns.

As soon as they got inside, Mercedes struggled to get down and ran to see the dogs. Carlo sank down on the bench beside the door, panting. Mercedes was tiny, but carrying her while breaking a trail had just about done him in.

"You're still sick," Fern scolded, standing in front of him. "You should probably be resting, not working."

"I'm fine, I just need a minute." Carlo wiped perspiration from his brow and staggered to his feet, calling to mind all the time he'd spent in battle under less than ideal physical circumstances. "What's the drill? Same as last night?"

Fern put a hand on her hip. Man, was she cute! "The drill is, you sit there and rest. Mercedes and I will feed the dogs."

"I'm a good helper," Mercedes called over from where she was squatting in front of a kennel, fingers poking in at the puppies inside.

"That's right, honey. But we never put our fingers in unless we're sure of our welcome."

Mercedes's lower lip poked out. "These ones are fine. You said."

"That's right. You're doing it just right."

Sunshine returned to the little girl's face and Carlo marveled at her mood shifts. Was that normal, or a product of losing her mom and changing homes? Or of whatever lifestyle Kath had put her through?

In any case, Fern seemed to handle his daughter beautifully. He wondered if he could do half as well.

"Oh, before I forget." Fern snapped her fingers and hurried over to the cage just next to the one where Mercedes was squatting. "We're supposed to check on this one mama dog. I got a text this morning."

"Pregnant?" Carlo asked. He was starting to catch his breath. Man, his stamina was totally gone after just a couple of weeks of this wretched tropical fever. But he needed to pull himself together and show he was a hard worker, a man who could protect and care for others. That was how he'd get custody of his daughter, not by wheezing on a bench like a ninety-year-old with lung disease.

"No, she's not pregnant. She had puppies and all but one died, so they put the one in with another litter to socialize it and…aw, Mama, you're lonely, aren't you?"

Carlo walked over to where Fern was kneeling and peered into the kennel. A large chocolate-brown dog lay in the back corner, head on paws.

"C'mere, come on, Brownie, I'll give you a biscuit," Fern coaxed, but the dog stayed down, emitting a low whine.

"That's not good. They said she needs to eat."

Fern frowned. "I wonder if it's good for her to be right next to her puppy like this. Where she can see her, but not be with her. That would be hard."

No kidding. Carlo found himself identifying with the mama dog. "Is she feeding the pup?"

"Apparently not." Fern nodded toward the next kennel, where five or six puppies played and rolled and nipped each other. "I guess that mama dog over there is feeding all of them. And they say it's better for a puppy to be with other pups, but I feel bad for poor Brownie."

"Mama Fern, look! The little one is hurt!" Mercedes's voice sounded distressed.

Both Fern and Carlo stepped over to where Mercedes knelt by the cage full of puppies. "Over there, Mama! Help him!"

In the corner of the cage, a small brown-and-white-spotted puppy lay alone. Carlo felt his heart constricting, looking at Mercedes's face, wondering if the little guy was dead and if so, how that would affect Mercedes. "Is there a flashlight?"

"Mercedes, run get our flashlight from the desk," Fern urged, kneeling to see the little dog. "He's not moving," she said to Carlo in a low voice.

"Here, Mama!" Mercedes handed the flashlight to Fern and she shone it on the puppy. Its eyes were closed, its breathing rapid, but at least there was breathing.

There were also a couple of open wounds on his side and back.

"Oh, wow, I don't know what to do," Fern said. "That's the one that doesn't belong. It looks like either the mama dog or the other pups have turned on him."

As if on cue, the chocolate-colored dog began to whine from the next kennel.

"Should we put him back with his mama?" Carlo asked.

"I don't know. Let me text the people who normally take care of them," Fern said. "And meanwhile, I'll get the others fed."

"I'll stay and watch over him," Mercedes offered.

"Okay, that will be great. I think Carlo will stay with you and help. Right?" Fern gave him a stern, meaningful stare.

"Um…okay." Man, this diminutive, shy librarian had a spine of steel. There was no disagreeing with her.

This time, Fern didn't linger with each dog, but moved rapidly from kennel to kennel, letting dogs out into the runs if they'd go, pouring food from large canisters. Carlo marveled at how hard she was capable of working, and he handled the dogs two or three kennels to either side of the problem dogs, trying to lighten her load while also keeping an eye on Mercedes, making sure she wasn't seeing something up-setting.

When Mercedes cried out, he was glad he'd stuck close. He rushed back over in time to see one of the other puppies jump on top of the spotted pup and nip at it. "He's hurting the little puppy," Mercedes cried. "Stop him!"

Carlo didn't know if it was normal puppy play or something more aggressive, but he could see that the little guy wasn't in any shape to play rough. "Step back, and I'll pull him out," he told Mercedes, and then he went in and picked up the puppy.

"Oh, no, oh, no, is he okay?"

"I don't know." He needed to keep Mercedes calm as well as help the pup. Which meant keeping her busy. "Can you find a towel we can wrap him in?"

Fern was all the way down at the other end of the kennel, so Carlo got Mercedes to help him wrap the puppy in the towel she'd found. "We'll be really careful," he said, watching Mercedes. His daughter. Wow.

"Mama Fern said kids can only touch a dog with two fingers, so you better hold him," Mercedes told Carlo gravely.

So he sat cross-legged on the floor and held

the dog, and Mercedes petted the pup with two fingers, and somehow she ended up sitting in his lap, leaning her head against his chest and chattering every thought that came into her four-year-old brain.

Just keep breathing, Carlo told himself.

No matter what happened, he'd have these moments with his daughter to cherish forever. He could enjoy the fruity smell of her hair and the pink of her cheeks and the confiding, sweet tone of her voice. He could look at her dark eyes and realize that those came from Kath, but her strong chin probably came from his side of the family. He got a sudden memory of his sister, Angelica, when she was small, and realized that Mercedes had her flat cheekbones and cute nose.

Fern came up behind them, a heavy bag of dog food in her arms, breathing hard. "Oh, man," she said, "you took him out. Is he okay?"

"I think he's going to be." Carlo looked up and tried to communicate with his eyes that he had no idea, but was putting a positive spin on things for Mercedes's sake. He felt like a cad for just sitting here while she worked, but on the other hand, he could clearly see that Mercedes needed nurturing. So maybe this was how you managed it with two parents—you dumped gender stereotypes and played which-ever role needed playing at the time.

Fern was studying her phone. "They said to take him out if he's being bullied, that some-times the rest of the litter turns on a puppy."

The sad mama dog came up to the front of the cage and sniffed and whined her agitation.

"Do you think she knows it's hers?" Angelica asked.

"Sure looks that way. What else did your friends say?"

"Oh, they're not my friends, they're just peo-ple who help out here. I don't…" She trailed off, waved a hand, leaving Carlo curious about what she'd been about to say. "Anyway, they said maybe we should take the mama and the pup up to the house, and see if she could still feed him some. Apparently, they just moved him over a day or two ago. She might still have her milk."

"We can have them at the house?" Mer-cedes jumped out of Carlo's lap and threw her arms around Fern. "I always wanted a puppy! What's his name, Mama Fern?"

"I don't think he has one yet." Fern stroked Mercedes's hair and there was such happiness and tenderness in her face that Carlo had to look away. "We'll think of something to call him, at least for now."

"His name is Spots," Mercedes announced. "'Cause he has spots!"

"Makes sense to me." Carlo got to his feet, bringing the pup with him. "If you carry the little one and I carry the mama…"

"Can you? She's huge."

He gave her a look and then opened the cage. "I can, unless she wants to walk. I don't know how her health is."

"And you hafta carry me," Mercedes reminded him.

"That's right." He patted her messy hair as warmth spread through his chest.

So they made their way back to the house in stages. Carlo carried the big dog while Mercedes and Fern worked in the kennel and watched the puppy. Then he went back to carry Mercedes while Fern brought the puppy and a bag of supplies.

By the time they got settled in the house again, he was sweating and dizzy, but he kept it together and brought in a bunch of wood and built a fire. Made sure the mama and puppy were settled, along with Fern and Mercedes. And then he collapsed onto the sofa.

He must have dozed off or even passed out, because Fern touched him and he jerked and then relaxed. Something in her touch was soothing.

"You made yourself sick again, didn't you?"

she scolded. "I heated up more soup. Sit up and eat it."

Carlo couldn't let her do this. Couldn't let himself accept the caretaking, especially when he knew that his only shot at Mercedes was being superman here. If he couldn't be superman, if he had to be weak, then he needed to hide it away. Along with his strange desire to reach up and touch Fern's cheek. "I'll just sleep it off in the den," he growled, and slunk away from the vulnerability and the weakness and the worry.

Fern watched him go, and the sense of rejection was enormous. Just like her to mess things up with Carlo. Of course he didn't want to spend time around her. She'd come on too strong with the nurturing, but what was she supposed to do? She was more used to being around kids and animals than adults. Kids and animals loved being taken care of.

A big manly man like Carlo was different, she supposed, and it was just her own awkwardness that had made her think she could take care of him, or that he'd want her to.

"Mama? What are we gonna do now?"

The plaintive voice pulled Fern out of her funk. It didn't matter what some strange man thought of her. She squatted down beside Mercedes, who was sitting cross-legged petting the little puppy. "You're doing just the right thing. I'm proud of you for being so gentle. You just keep doing that while I text the caretakers and find out what to do next."

Although Fern could see now that Brownie's ribs showed, her demeanor was much happier. She wasn't whining anymore, just licking her puppy as if to make up for the time apart.

Minutes later Fern's phone buzzed and she read the instructions, still sitting with her arm around Mercedes. "Okay, they say we're supposed to get the mama dog something to eat. Even if she's nursing, we should put some soft food nearby so she can eat whenever she needs to and get her milk back up."

"What's the puppy doing?"

Fern watched as the puppy nuzzled at the mama dog's teats and took a deep breath. Okay, time for a new mothering challenge. "Mama dogs feed their pups from their bodies. The dog has a nipple like a baby bottle, and milk comes out of it."

"That's silly! That's not where milk comes from."

"Nope, but our milk comes from cows."

Mercedes's nose wrinkled. "I don't drink from a cow!"

Fern chuckled. "No, but the cow gets milked

by the farmer, and then the milk gets sent to the grocery store, and then we buy it and drink it." She hesitated. "When you were a baby, you drank from your mama just like that little puppy." She didn't want to upset Mercedes, but the social worker had told her it was good to refer to her biological mother naturally, in conversation. That way, Mercedes would know that her mother and her experiences with her mother weren't a taboo subject.

"I drank from my mommy?" Mercedes asked wonderingly.

"Yes, your mommy told me she breast-fed you for a whole year. She loved you so much."

"Yeah." Mercedes looked thoughtful for a minute. "Hey, the puppy is biting the mommy!"

Fern was watching, too. The puppy was obviously getting some sustenance, but even to her inexperienced eye, it looked like a struggle. "Tell you what, let's get Brownie that food. Maybe she needs more to eat before she can feed her pup." She sincerely hoped Brownie could feed the pup entirely, both because it was better for the little guy, and because she didn't know exactly how they'd manage the frequent feedings a little puppy would need.

"What will she eat?"

"I guess she'll eat Bull's food." Suddenly,

Fern realized she hadn't seen the old bulldog. "Where is Bull anyway?"

"Mr. Carlo took him in the den. He said it was better if they didn't meet yet, because they might fight."

"Okay." She had to appreciate Carlo's practical help. The man was just…capable, and it was a relief to have him here even though he made her uncomfortable.

After Brownie had eaten and settled down with a big doggy sigh, her pup beside her, Fern and Mercedes played board games in front of the fire. Mercedes had a snack and took a short nap, and Fern seized the opportunity to work a little on her picture book.

When Mercedes got up, she distracted her with half an hour of television so she could work a little more and finish her ideas. A small flash of guilt about that, but after all, it was a snow day and half an hour of TV wasn't too bad. Mercedes normally went to day care while Fern worked, and she was used to structure and varied activities in her day.

What else was she going to do with little Mercy? She put her paints away and then wandered into the kitchen. Outside the windows, the sun peeked through clouds on its way to a beautiful sunset, all pink and peachy and orange and purple. Snow was heaped high against the fence line and the barn. Trees raised spidery arms into the sky, and the beauty was breathtaking. Yes, she had to do a winter story soon just so she could capture some of this in her art.

She daydreamed of Ezra Scott Keats and *The Snowy Day*. They didn't own the picture book, but she'd checked it out several times from the library. She looked through Angelica's various shelves of picture books and found that one, along with several others related to snow.

She and Mercedes lay down by the fire for a little while, reading, but it was clearly not active enough for the little girl and she got fidgety. So Fern pulled out her big guns. "Want to bake cookies?"

"Yeah!" Mercedes's eyes glowed. "Can we really?"

"Sure. Let's go find all the ingredients. I'm sure Angelica has everything basic." It was true; as the mother of a first-grader, Angelica kept her kitchen well stocked in chocolate chips.

As they mixed together the dough, as she showed Mercedes what to do and let her help, Fern flashed back to one memorable day in her favorite foster home, where Granny Jentis had let two of the girls help her bake cookies. It had been just such a snowy day. They'd baked batch after batch of sugar cookies and Fern remembered the thrill of licking the spoon and of watching the sticky dough turn into delicious warm cookies.

If she had her way, Mercedes would have many, many days like that: homey, family days.

Sudden fear flashed through her. What if things didn't work out? What if something happened in the adoption process and Mercedes couldn't stay?

She drew in a deep breath. Glanced over reflexively at the verse Angelica had hung on the kitchen wall: "There is no fear in love; but perfect love casts out fear."

Angelica was a good Christian. The whole family was. And the thought of enough love to rid yourself of fear was amazing.

Fern didn't have that. She wished she did, and she knew from church that many believers had such faith that fear was gone or greatly diminished. That would be wonderful. Now, with so much more than she'd ever had to lose, Fern wished fervently that she had that safe, loving, loved feeling.

She didn't. And with her background, she didn't know if she ever would.

But she loved Mercedes with all her heart, and all she could do was to focus on that love.

They were pulling the first batch of cookies

out of the oven when Carlo came in, rubbing his stubbly face. In his faded jeans and loose sweater, sleeves pushed up to reveal brawny forearms, he looked impossibly handsome, and Fern's heart rate shot up just looking at him.

Which was weird, because she *never* went mushy and boy-crazy like other women.

"Smells great in here," he said, sounding calmer and more cheerful than before. "What's going on?"

"We baked cookies!" Mercedes shouted, her voice joyous. "I never did it before, and Mama Fern says I'm really good at it."

"Hmm." Carlo bent over the cookie tray Fern was holding, pretending to sniff the cookies. His nearness just about took Fern's breath away, weirdly enough. "I'm not sure. Would you like me to be a cookie tester for you?"

Fern whirled away and set the cookies down on a pot holder on the counter. "He's trying to fool us, Mercy. He wants the first taste of a cookie, but you're the one who gets that."

Mercedes studied him carefully. "He can try it," she said finally. "I like him."

Carlo took a hot cookie, bit into it and licked the crumb off his lip. His eyes sparkled at Fern. "Hmm," he said. "That was…" He knelt in front of Mercedes. "The very best cookie I ever tasted!"

"I know, and this is the very best day I ever had!" Mercedes's eyes widened then. "Except I wish Mommy was here."

Fern squatted down and hugged the little girl. "Your mama would be so proud of you for all your hard work today," she said.

There was a yip from the corner, sounding as if one of the dogs was barking approval, and Carlo looked over. "How are they doing?"

When they all went over to check, the puppy was nursing contentedly while the older dog lay on her side.

"Mama Fern, she's smiling!" Mercedes cried.

"It looks that way. I think she's happy to be with her pup."

Indignant yowling came from the room where Carlo had been sleeping. "Sounds like old Bull isn't happy to be left out," Carlo said.

"Do you think we should put them together?"

"Not yet, but maybe later tonight. Bull seems like a nice guy, but this is his territory and—"

A loud *pop* interrupted him.

All the lights went out.

Chapter Five

⌒

"Whoa!" Carlo tensed instantly and reached for the spot where he'd last seen Mercedes, but his hand brushed Fern's hip instead and he jerked it back.

"Mama!" Mercedes cried, and he sensed rather than saw Fern kneeling beside her.

"Shh, sweets, it's okay. Mama Fern's here." She directed her voice toward him. "What happened?"

"Must be from the storm." He had pretty good night vision and spatial memory, so he made his way across the room and opened the window shades.

Sunset had turned the sky purple and orange and pink, but he couldn't see any electrical lights outside, not even way in the distance where another farm was usually visible. The outage must be widespread.

Behind him, Mercedes's scared sniffling turned into a wail.

"I'm right here, Mercy." Fern's voice was calm, even upbeat. "Looks as if we're going to have a little adventure."

"I don't like dark," the child cried.

Carlo fumbled in his pocket for the flashlight that was always on his key chain. In a minute, its feeble beam was joined by a stronger one from Fern's phone. "There we go," he said. "Light and an adventure."

As had become automatic in his missionary work, he sent up a quick prayer. *Unexpected stuff here, Lord, but not to You. Help us.*

"Wonder where Troy and Angelica keep the candles," Fern mused. She'd stood and was cuddling Mercedes on her hip.

"No dark," the little girl sobbed.

"Shh, it's going to be okay. We'll have fun."

"No, 'cause lights cost money. And we can't get them back for a long time."

Her words smote Carlo. Kath and Mercedes must have gone without electricity. Without intending to, he'd neglected his own child to the point where she'd lacked the physical necessities of life.

He'd lived up to every bad expectation he'd heard growing up. That Camden boy. Always in trouble. Won't amount to anything.

Fern's voice, sweet and calm, brought him back to the present. "Oh, no, Mercy, the reason the power went out is the storm. No big deal. The lights will come back on as soon as the workers can fix the electrical lines."

Mercedes lifted her head. "Can we still make the cookies?" she asked plaintively.

"Um...no. The oven won't work without power."

"But I want to bake the cookies!"

"Shh!" Fern sounded frustrated and a little scared. "We've got a lot to think about."

Hearing the anxiety in Fern's voice made Carlo's training snap into place. *Take charge.* "First thing, we're all okay." He injected total confidence into the words as he put a hand on Fern's shoulder and a hand on Mercedes's. "That's most important. Next issue is the dogs. How are our guys in here?"

As he'd hoped, the thought of the dogs stopped Mercedes's crying, which had to take a load of stress off Fern.

He was rewarded by her grateful smile. "Can you help me check them out, Mercy?" she asked, and they all walked over to examine the mama and puppy.

True to canine form, the two appeared to be completely relaxed. But when Carlo shone his light on the pup, he noticed that its sores looked raw. "Did your friends say what to do about these?"

"They said they'd heal unless the pup or mama get obsessive about licking them."

Just then, Brownie lifted her head and started licking her puppy's back.

"Hmm." To Carlo, the wounds looked worse, and then a memory came back to him. "I have an idea about how to stop her from licking. Mind if I try?"

Even in the dim light he could see Fern's concerned frown. "How much do you know about dogs?"

Good for her. The dogs were her responsibility and she couldn't let just anyone take charge of them. He lifted his hands. "Believe me, I'm no veterinarian. But I did spend a week on a farm one time and something similar was going on with a mama cow and a calf."

"And you fixed it?"

"No, I watched a very experienced farmer fix it, and it worked."

She scratched behind the mama dog's ears and looked up at him. "In Central America? And if it was a farm, must've been during the missionary years?"

He stared at her. "You really pay attention."

"That's the benefit of us quiet types." Her slow smile made his heart skip a beat.

They were all kneeling around the sleepy pair of dogs. Carlo could see the furniture as dark shapes, and outside the window, the moon was just starting to rise. When he leaned away from the dogs and toward Fern, he noticed her light floral perfume.

"As long as it doesn't hurt the dogs." She bit her lip, her face suddenly scrunched with worry, and he couldn't help it—he reached out a hand and smoothed the lines from her fore-head.

Which made her go very, very still.

"Hey," he said to calm the fear in those huge eyes. And to calm his own suddenly racing heart. "I want the dogs to stay safe, too. I don't want to hurt them, okay? You can trust me."

Even as he said it, his stomach turned over. Because yeah, she could trust him about the dogs, but what about her and Mercedes? Wasn't he keeping the biggest secret of all from them?

She blinked behind those glasses, smiled and nodded. "Okay, farmer Carlo. Do your stuff."

Man, was she cute when she tried to be funny. Apparently, Mercedes thought so, too, because she chortled with laughter. "He's not a farmer, Mama Fern! He's a soldier!"

Carlo was standing up to get what he needed from the kitchen, but at those words, he stiff-ened. "Who told her that?"

Fern lifted her hands, palms up. "Not me. How'd you know, Mercy?"

"I guessed a secret!" Mercedes crowed. "'Cause he's like the movies Mommy watched at night."

"There you go, Rambo," Fern said drily.

He turned away, using his flashlight to guide him toward the kitchen. He was trying to leave his mercenary days behind, trying to atone for them, actually, but it seemed he couldn't shed the stink of war. Nor the things he'd done there.

Oh, he'd been on the right side, fighting for the common people against dictators who committed atrocities and ruined lives. But you couldn't help getting some blood on your hands, and as time had gone by, it had haunted him more, not less.

He shook off the thoughts and found lemon and red pepper and salt. Mixed them into a paste in a bowl, making sure the amount of red pepper was much less than his farmer friend would have used, figuring a puppy's skin was more tender than a calf's. And then he carried it out and spread a little near the cut.

The mama dog was curious, but even one whiff of his concoction made her turn away, snorting.

"Hey," Fern protested. "What if she rejects the puppy now?"

"Let's just watch. Mamas are protective. They'll go against their best interest to take care of their young."

Boy, did he hope he was right! He'd gotten attached to the little pup, and he felt responsible for it. Not only that, but he wanted to shove the skepticism off Fern's face, to replace it with admiration. Fortunately, for now at least, the dog kept the puppy close to her side and allowed him to nurse.

Carlo did the evening feed of the kennel dogs himself, brushing aside Fern's offer to go out with him. He needed a few minutes away. He needed to think.

Was he doing the right thing, not telling Fern the truth about his connection to Mercedes?

She'd be angry if he told her now, that was for sure. She might kick him right out into the snowstorm.

If she did that, he'd be fine, he'd manage, but what would happen to her and Mercedes? With shaky electricity and phone service and a barn full of dogs to take care of, they needed help. He was more and more impressed with Fern's self-reliance and independent spirit, but even she had her limits. Taking care of a farm and a bunch of dogs and a little girl in these conditions was much more than a one-woman job.

When he went back inside, the relief on

her face made him feel ten feet tall, and more certain that he was right to keep things calm, keep controversial stuff to himself, while they needed him.

He noticed that the floor was strewn with toys, mostly action figures and little plastic soldiers and dinosaurs. A box of juice lay on its side next to a dark, damp spot on the carpet. "You okay?"

"I'm okay," she said, pushing her glasses up her nose, "but Mercy's got issues. She's still a little scared of the dark, and after you left, it got worse. It's because of stuff she went through with her mom. And to top that off, she's easily frustrated, and I... Well, I caved and let her watch a video on my phone. It's stupid, because we need to save the charge, since the landline gets glitchy in storms, but I didn't know what else to do."

"She had a meltdown?"

She nodded. "They can come on suddenly. Again, it's a function of her background. Kath was honest with me about how she wasn't the best at parenting throughout Mercedes's younger years. There was poverty and some drug use, and Mercedes didn't always get comforted right away. That affects a kid."

Once again, guilt washed over Carlo. He should have been there, helping, maybe even taking custody of Mercedes if Kath wasn't able to handle her care. If only he'd known.

"So anyway, she's upset right now because she never made cookies before, if you can believe it, and now we can't because of the stove."

He took a breath and did what he'd been trained to do: let the past go, focus on now. There was a lot in Mercedes's history he couldn't fix, but this was one thing he could. "I have an idea," he said. "We can rig something up to bake cookies using the fireplace. Want to help me try?"

She cocked her head to one side, a slight smile making her look flirtatious. "Are you really that handy?"

"Let's just say I've spent a lot of time improvising. Do you have any tinfoil?"

They used his flashlight to go through the dark kitchen cupboards, finding what they needed. They were fortunate to stumble onto an oil lamp, too, half-full. Once that was lit, Carlo carried it out to where Mercedes huddled under a blanket on the couch, clutching Fern's phone. He set the oil lamp on the hearth above, well out of the child's reach—you couldn't be too careful with kids and fire.

"Okay," Fern said, carrying the rest of the supplies out to the fireplace. "Do your best."

"Hey, Mercy, want to stop watching the

video and help me build an oven?" He needed to save the charge on that phone. His own phone was next to worthless, and they had to be able to get in touch with the outside world for emergency purposes. The landline had been out when he'd checked.

Carlo fooled around with baking sheets and tinfoil while Mercedes watched. Finally, he had something he thought would work. "Bring those cookies, women!" he jokingly commanded.

Fern flashed him a fake scowl. "Neanderthal," she shot at him before rising effortlessly to her feet from a cross-legged position and taking Mercedes to the kitchen.

Mercedes seemed to have forgotten her fear of the dark, and the dogs slept peacefully, and Carlo felt calm descend over him. *Thank You, Lord*, he whispered as he looked around the lamp-lit room.

So many times he'd been in places where weather and illness and violence had made life awful. Here was the softer side, the reason he'd fought for his country. Here was the home that he'd not had while growing up.

Angelica had done herself proud, creating such a wonderful environment for herself and her child, pushing through all the barriers to a relationship that came from the way they'd been raised. He was proud of his little sister, and happy for her, too. She practically glowed through the phone when she talked about her new husband. And as Fern and Mercedes came back into the room, Mercedes carefully carrying a tray of cookies to bake, he had a moment of wishing he might get some of that glow, that joy, for himself.

This won't last. Fern will be furious when she finds out.

But just for this one night, he was going to pretend.

So they put the cookies in the makeshift convection oven. Carlo had no clue about how long it would take—he was anything but a chef—but whatever the baking time, he figured it would be too long for a four-year-old. "Want to let Bull out?" he asked Mercedes. "The old guy's got to be lonely in there."

"Yeah!" she yelled, and ran to the door.

"Hold on." He raised a hand, his voice automatically taking on the tone of command, and she turned around, eyes wide. "Don't touch that door. We want to get the mama and pup ready."

"You guard them while I help Mercedes get Bull," Fern said. She was lifting an eyebrow at him, her expression cool, and suddenly he knew she was thinking he'd overstepped his bounds, that he shouldn't think he could tell everyone what to do.

"Hey, I'm used to being in charge, what can I say?" He spread his hands and grinned at her.

"I noticed." One hand on her hip, she lifted her chin. Yeah, a woman to be reckoned with.

"I'm keeping her entertained, right?" he challenged her.

She frowned another second, considering, and then chuckled. "Yes, you are, and I'm grateful. Just…not used to sharing the spotlight." As she said it, a surprised expression crossed her face.

"What's wrong?"

"I normally hate having other people around!" Then she clapped a hand to her mouth. "That came out wrong. It's just that, I'm an introvert. Kids and animals I can hang with all day, but I usually find adults to be pretty exhausting."

"But not me?" He kept his eyes locked on hers.

"You can be…annoying, but not exhausting." She said the words slowly, and her eyes widened, and she blew out a breath. "This is freaking me out." And she turned around to where Mercedes was waiting at the living room door.

She wasn't the only one freaked out. Carlo

hadn't ever been this comfortable around a woman. Or actually, his agitated inability to take his eyes off Fern wasn't what he'd call comfortable. But he wanted to stick with her. Wanted to protect and help her. Didn't want this private interlude to end.

"Here he comes! Look out!" Mercedes cried as Bull raced into the room, moving with surprising agility on his three legs.

He saw the other two dogs and skidded to a halt.

A low growl came from Brownie's chest, and her hackles rose.

Bull lumbered toward the pair and Carlo watched the dogs closely. In battle, he'd learned to trust his instincts, and he was relying on them now. If a fight started, he'd have to move fast.

Bull reached the mother dog and she stood, moving in front of the puppy. There was still that little growl, maybe a whine, coming from her chest.

And then Bull's stub of a tail started to wag. He sniffed the mama dog and then pushed past her to the pup, and she let him. He sniffed the little one and then jerked his head away from the ointment on the pup's back. Then the old bulldog plopped down on the floor beside their bed, letting out a massive doggy sigh.

"He likes them!" Mercedes said. "Oh, Bull, you're such a good dog! I wish we could have a dog, Mama Fern," she added as a calculating expression came into her eyes.

"That's something to think about." Fern winked at Carlo and he about melted.

"The cookies!" Mercedes cried, and Fern hurried over to check. They pulled them out just in time.

And for all their half burned, half baked gooiness, they were the best cookies Carlo had ever had.

The house got progressively colder—even a gas furnace wouldn't operate without electricity—so they stuck close to the fire. After they'd scrounged for a little dinner and read several storybooks, Fern went upstairs and came down with an armload of blankets. "It's warmest here, so we'll kind of camp out like a pioneer family," she explained to Mercedes as she spread blankets out on the floor.

"And he's like the daddy!" Mercedes pointed at Carlo.

Fern laughed. "Yes, he's like the daddy."

Carlo's conscience nudged him. *Like* nothing. He *was* the daddy.

And here was maybe the only time he'd get to spend with his daughter, so he was going to make the best of it. He got up and helped Fern create a giant nest on the hearth rug. Soon, Mercedes, safe in between the two grown-ups, was yawning in the glow of the fire.

"Tell me the story about the princess," she begged Fern.

"But you've heard it a thousand times. And Carlo doesn't want to hear it."

"Oh, yes, I do." Anything to keep her talking in that quiet, slightly husky voice, and to watch the lamplight glow golden on the hair of his little girl.

It was like something right out of Laura Ingalls Wilder. It was them against nature, their little family against the world. He listened to Fern's story of a princess who had one mama watching over her in heaven and one taking care of her on earth, and marveled at how she nurtured his little girl. Marveled that God had worked so much for good.

He didn't want the moment to stop. And when Mercedes's eyes closed, her lashes dark against flushed cheeks, he wanted to lean over and kiss her forehead, but that might be too weird.

And who was he kidding? He wanted to kiss Fern, too. But that, for sure, he didn't dare to do. "Sleep tight, you two," he said, and made his way to the cold, lonely couch in the next room.

Chapter Six

The next day Fern got out her watercolors and sat at her easel in front of the big picture window. But her eyes couldn't stay on her work. She kept getting distracted by the scene outside.

The day had dawned bright and sunny, but not as cold, and blessedly, the electricity had come back on sometime during the night. There was snow everywhere, and it was above her knees when they'd gone out to feed the dogs at sunrise.

And now Carlo had taken Mercedes outside to build a snowman. "Mama Fern needs some time to herself," he'd said cheerfully after breakfast.

How had he known that?

"So," he'd continued, looking only at Mercedes, "you and I are going to build the biggest snowman in the state of Ohio."

"Yay!"

Fern had felt a moment's hesitation, letting him take Mercedes out. Caring for the child was *her* job. But somehow, the situation felt right, if very strange. Her, Fern Easton, nerd extraordinaire, stranded here with a beautiful little girl and a giant, attractive soldier who normally wouldn't give her the time of day. Stranded, and spending time together like a family.

She'd never in her life felt part of a family. As early as she could remember, she'd known she was the extra, the foster kid, the one on the outside. Even in families that had lots of foster kids, she'd been the quiet one nobody had chosen to play with.

Now she knew it made sense; she'd gone into foster care grieving the loss of her parents, and so any ability she had to attach would have needed to be gently drawn out. She could hear echoes of her own history in Mercedes sometimes, how touchy grief was when the loss of a mother was involved, how it kept re-emerging with different events and reminders. From her reading, she knew that the cycle would continue throughout Mercedes's childhood: good months, and then plunging back into sadness again as she reached a new developmental stage.

Fern hadn't had a consistent, understanding caregiver in childhood, so she'd gone inside herself. And yeah, it had damaged her, to the point where she was terminally awkward with people and had only a few friends. Though some part of her longed for love and connection, she knew a warm family life wasn't in the cards for her.

Books had been her consolation and her friends, sometimes her only friends. They still were.

And thinking of books, she needed to concentrate on hers, she scolded herself. She'd been looking forward to this vacation time for ages, as an opportunity to work on the book she was contracted to do. Things hadn't gone as planned, at all, but right at this moment, she had a caregiver for her child and she had time to work. She'd best take advantage of it.

But the scene outside kept tugging at her.

Carlo and Mercedes were working together to lift the second giant snowball on top of the first one. Actually, Carlo was working and Mercedes was being more of a hindrance than a help, like any self-respecting four-year-old. She grabbed the snowball too tight and a big chunk broke off.

But Carlo didn't get mad. He laughed, set what remained of the snowball on top of the first and showed Mercedes how to pack extra snow into the hole she'd created.

He was a patient man, surprisingly patient. In her experience, most dads couldn't handle the antics and illogic and roller-coaster emotions of a preschooler, not as well as moms could. And someone like Carlo, obviously accustomed to the world of men, should have been totally out of his element.

Instead, he seemed amazingly comfortable with Mercedes. He seemed to truly care about her.

Watching them together, seeing their laughing faces, Fern frowned. There was something…some connection…

She shook off the thought, forced her attention back to her work and managed to get an illustration finished. And then, when her thoughts drifted once more to the scene outside the window, she gave up. Gathering a few supplies, she pulled on her warm jacket and went out to help them with the snowman.

"Mama!" Mercedes screamed when she saw Fern. "Look what we did! He's the biggest snowman in the whole state!"

"I think you might be right," Fern said, because the snow giant did indeed stand as tall as Carlo. "But I think he needs eyes and a nose, don't you?"

When she produced a carrot for a nose and chocolate sandwich cookies for eyes, Mercedes was ecstatic and of course, she had to place them herself. So Fern lifted her up while Carlo steadied the snowman. "How about a scarf?" he offered, and removed the plaid one he'd taken from the closet.

His coat was open and his head bare, and he wasn't shivering; he looked white toothed and handsome, and Fern's heart gave a little lurch. This was dangerous stuff. Dangerous, and not for her. She couldn't trust a man like that, and she certainly couldn't interest him. She turned away, feeling suddenly awkward.

And was rewarded with a snowball smacking her in the leg.

"Mama Fern, he threw a snowball at you!" Mercedes cried. "I want to do that, too!"

"No way!" She spun, not wanting...something. For Mercedes to play rough. For Carlo to tease. For them to have fun together as the family that they weren't.

"C'mon, Mercy, I'll help you," Carlo offered.

Fern opened her mouth to protest, but Carlo silenced her with a look. Which was a great trait for a military commander, but supremely annoying in a houseguest.

"But," he continued, "you have to follow

the rules of snowballs. Do you know what they are?"

"I didn't know there were rules," Mercedes said, wide-eyed.

"There are. You can't throw a snowball at a person's head or face. And when they say stop, you have to stop."

Yeah, yeah, Mr. Controlling. Fern took advantage of his distraction to land a snowball in the middle of Carlo's back.

"Hey!" In a flash he'd leaned down, scooped and formed a snowball and lobbed it at her. "Don't mess with a soldier, lady!"

"Me, me, I want to do it!" Mercedes cried, jumping up and down, and Carlo helped her form a snowball and throw it.

In for a penny, in for a pound. Fern wasn't going to be able to stop the battle, so she worked out her mixed feelings toward Carlo with a fierce barrage of snowballs, tossing the occasional lob in Mercedes's direction to keep the child happy. And she *was* happy; Fern loved the pink of Mercedes's cheeks and the sparkle in her eyes.

Mercedes hadn't had a man in her life, not much. According to Kath, there had been a few boyfriends, but no one who'd lived in or stuck around.

Seeing the way Mercedes acted with Carlo,

her excitement, her tiny flirtations—and seeing the confident, physical way he played with her—Fern realized the benefits a male influence could provide.

Unfortunately, it wasn't in the cards for her to marry and provide that influence. She was just too shy with men.

Unless... Except...

No. This was temporary. God had provided her with so much, giving her Mercedes. She couldn't expect, didn't deserve, any more. She'd have to solve the problem of a male influence for Mercedes another way.

Carlo hated to do it, but he turned on the television when they got inside. They'd been out of touch with the outside world for the better part of the day, but it was only right that he check and find out the weather forecast. They needed to know how long they'd be stranded and, if necessary, ration the supplies that were starting to run low.

"Looks as if we'll get some winds and drifting tonight," the local weatherman was saying, "but the winter storm itself seems to be over. And around Ohio, the hardest-hit rural communities are starting to dig themselves out."

"Good news," Carlo made himself say to

Fern. "Looks as if we may have one more night, max, before the plows get through."

"That's…great," she said with enthusiasm that sounded forced. Making him wonder if she was enjoying their isolation, at least the slightest little bit.

"Can we have hot chocolate?" Mercedes asked. "And more cookies?"

"Sure," Fern said, smiling at Mercedes.

Trust a kid to stay in the present and remember what was important: hot chocolate after a stint of playing outdoors.

And trust a woman like Fern to know how to do hot chocolate right: in big mugs, with leftover Christmas candy canes for stirrers and big dollops of marshmallow crème.

"Let's watch TV!" Mercedes cried as Fern carried the mugs toward the front room, where the fireplace was.

Fern narrowed her eyes. "Let's read a book *and* watch TV," she proposed. "Which do you want to do first?"

"TV, TV," Mercedes begged, and Fern frowned, cocking her head to one side.

"You can take the woman out of her library, but you can't really take the library out of the woman," Carlo said.

A smile tugged at the corners of her mouth. "Showing my true colors."

"You're good for her," Carlo said. "But there's nothing wrong with a movie now and then."

"Not if we all watch together," Fern said. "And not if it's—" she studied the shelf of DVDs "—*March of the Penguins*!" She held up the case triumphantly.

"Not a documentary!" Carlo scanned the shelf, knowing his sister would have his favorite movie. "How about *A Christmas Story*? I always wanted a Red Ryder BB gun!"

"Let me see that. A gun? And a PG rating? I don't think so."

And though he fake begged and pleaded, Fern wouldn't back down. And she got Mercedes to vote with her by challenging her to walk like a penguin. And pretty soon they were all doing it, and laughing, and Carlo was giving in.

Truthfully, he didn't much care what movie it was, when he could watch it with this woman and this child and a delicious mug of hot chocolate.

And pretend the world outside wasn't really waiting for them.

Chapter Seven

Hours later, Fern came downstairs after putting Mercedes to bed. It was dark outside, but way too early to fall asleep, and she felt a sudden sense of trepidation.

The scene in front of her felt scarily intimate. Like one of a million old movies she'd seen.

Slowly, she walked into the room. Fireplace… check. Furry hearth rug…check. Low light… check. Snowstorm outside…check. Handsome man smiling at her…check.

It was a setting for romance, and she knew exactly what was supposed to happen next. Even she herself was a stereotype: the shy librarian who'd take her glasses off and let her hair down and become a beautiful, passionate, at-ease woman.

Except that was where the movie shut down; that was the page missing from the romance novel. She *wasn't* a secretly passionate and beautiful woman waiting to be unleashed.

She stomped in and sat down on the fur rug. It was itchy, and the fire felt hot. She couldn't see anything in the low light. "I can't wait to get out of here," she said, and looked at Carlo defiantly. If he had some other expectation, just because there'd been a few sparks between them, he was going to be disappointed.

Carlo looked at her strangely. "Really?"

"Yeah, really." She knew she sounded hostile, but it was better than pathetic. "Don't you want to leave?" She figured he was dying to. He'd been kind to stay, but a man like Carlo had a million more exciting things to do than hang with the likes of her.

"No, I don't." He shifted onto his side and propped his head on his elbow. "I'm in no hurry at all for the plows to get through." He leaned back on his elbows and smiled at her.

That smile warmed her face and chest, making her wish for things that women like her never got. She looked away. "I can't wait," she repeated. "I'm going crazy stuck in here."

"Because…"

"It's too hot!" She scooted away from the fire.

Carlo raised an eyebrow. "Take something off."

"Oh, please." She tried to sound casual, sophisticated, like the women he must be used to. Inside, his suggestion made her heart flutter like a caged bird.

He reached out and touched her arm and she jerked violently away.

"I just meant you have about six layers on." He regarded her with a cryptic expression.

Heat rose in her cheeks. She'd misinterpreted his remark as flirting, thinking he might be a little bit attracted to her, especially since there was no one else around.

She reached for safer ground, a change of subject. "So since we have some time," she said, "why don't you tell me about your adventures in Central America?"

His eyebrows lifted, and he looked surprised and a little uncomfortable. *So there, buddy, I'm turning the tables on you.*

"That's not very good entertainment." He sat forward and poked at the fire. "Maybe we should just turn on the game."

As if to disallow that possibility, at that moment the power snapped off again. The room, suddenly dark, seemed to shrink to the circle of two in the fire's low light.

"Must be the rising temperatures," Carlo said. "Makes for heavy snow on trees and power lines." He stood and fumbled for the matches and lit the lamp, which cast its soft glow over the room.

"Hopefully, it won't stay off for as long this time," she said. In reality, she welcomed the dim light, where Carlo couldn't see her embarrassment, or whatever other feelings he stirred in her. "Guess that rules out TV, and you'll have to entertain me."

"Oh, really?"

"By telling me about your adventures." She was back on steady ground now; she'd turned the tables and felt in control. The romantic situation was firmly squashed down, and she could do what she did best: listening.

"Why don't you tell me about you?" he asked, flopping down on his back with a kind of pleading in his voice.

"Nope. Nothing ever happens to me. How come you decided to go to Central America?"

He was silent for a minute, but she let him be, sensing the reason was complicated. Finally, he spoke. "I was looking for a way to use what I'd learned in the army, and make money, and get away from Rescue River. And I was kind of an adrenaline junkie."

"Why doesn't that surprise me?" But she smiled. She could imagine a younger Carlo, restless, wanting to do big things.

"I heard about an outfit that was helping out

down there. Found out I had some sharpshooter skills they needed. The rest..." Through the dim room, she could see him lift his hands. "The rest just played out."

"Did you like it?"

"What, Central America?"

"Fighting. Being a soldier."

Firelight flickered across his face, and a log shifted and burst, sending out sparks and a crackling sound. Fern grabbed a pillow from the couch and put it under her head. Now the fur rug didn't feel scratchy to her, just soft and warm. "Was it...fun? Exciting?"

He let out a dry laugh. "Aah. No. Nobody really likes being a soldier."

"But that's not true. A lot of people are proud of being in the military. Or...paramilitary, whatever it was with you."

"It was both, and being proud of it and liking it are two different things. I'm proud of some of the things we were able to accomplish, but..." He shook his head and shifted, a rustling movement in the dark room. "There's a lot you don't want to know about."

"People do want to know. At the library, military memoirs are getting more popular all the time."

"Especially if they sugarcoat the truth. The

only audience that can take the true story are other vets."

"Maybe." She waited, but he obviously wasn't going to talk any more about that. And as a sheltered American who'd benefitted immensely from all that the armed forces had done for her, who was she to argue?

On the other hand, she did want to keep him talking, so things wouldn't go all romantic. So she could stay in control. And most guys loved to talk about themselves. Carlo didn't seem to be fitting that stereotype, but maybe she just hadn't found the right topic. "So why did you become a missionary?"

"Can't we talk about something else? Why did you become a librarian?"

"Because I love books. Why'd you become a missionary?"

He lifted himself up onto his side again and even in the dim light of the fire, she knew he was looking at her. "You're a persistent little thing, aren't you?"

"I've been called…stubborn. Why don't you want to talk about it?" Oh, she was on a roll now. If she could just keep him on edge and talking about himself, he wouldn't try to make some horribly awkward or obligatory move on her. They could both be spared that.

"I can talk about it," he said, "if you're really interested."

"I am."

"Okay, then," he said. "I found Jesus, or rather, He found me."

She leaned toward him, curious. "No atheists in foxholes? Or was it more than that?" She'd had her own, quiet moment of conversion, but a part of her wished for fireworks.

He gave her a wry smile. "I'm sure that's part of it, but no. I think God chases us all our lives. I think He wants us to live His way."

Had God sought her? Fern tucked that away for further consideration. "And being a soldier wasn't His way?"

"Well." He sighed. "Let's just say there was a better way."

He was glossing over the story, she could tell. "I don't believe you."

He sat up straighter. "What?"

"You make it sound all pretty," she said, "but I suspect there's a lot more to the story. And that it's not all cut-and-dried."

"You calling me a liar?"

"No, no. Just a…a whitewasher. Like, why'd you have a knife and practically battle armor in your bag if you're just a sweet innocent missionary now?"

His eyes narrowed just a little. "Being a

missionary doesn't mean having life easy. I've probably been in more dangerous situations as a missionary than I was as a soldier. But as long as we're making accusations... I think you're a distractor. I think you want to keep me talking so I don't think about and talk about you."

She picked at a spot on the wooden floor, not looking at him. "What do you mean?"

"I mean," he said, "that you sit over there on the other side of the fireplace with your arms wrapped around your knees, telling me I'm not truthful enough. It keeps the focus off you, and you like it that way."

She couldn't help smiling at how well he'd read her. "Touché. It's working, isn't it?"

His eyes glowed in the firelight, holding hers, and suddenly there was a whole lot more tension in the room. So much so that it felt overwhelming.

"Tell me about your call to be a missionary," she said.

"Why?"

She shrugged. "I'm curious, that's all."

"Why?"

"Because..." She thought about it. "Because God hasn't called me and I want to know what it's like."

"Okay." Apparently satisfied by her answer,

he leaned back and cradled his head in his arms, staring up at the ceiling. "It was as if… I couldn't get away. I didn't have peace. I felt Him telling me He wanted to use me. Not in words, but…in thoughts. It was weird."

Fern felt oddly jealous. "Yeah?"

"Yeah. So I'd go into the next village and do what my job required, and I kept thinking, do they know Jesus, have they had the chance? It got to be an obsession. The first thing I'd do is look around, see if anyone had a cross hanging on the wall or a Bible beside their bed."

"And if they didn't?"

"If they didn't, well, no matter how horrible they were being, I couldn't do anything to put them at risk of death. I couldn't contribute to anyone dying unsaved."

"Must have cramped your style as a mercenary."

"Exactly!" He chuckled. "I don't think anyone's ever asked me about this stuff before. It was as if God was pushing me out of fighting for justice and into saving souls."

Fern turned over on her side to see him better and her heart fluttered again. Man, she'd better look out, because she could really fall for this guy. He was good and sincere and manly, not to mention super handsome. His words mesmerized her. A scene from her favorite Shakespeare play flashed into her mind: Othello, the older war general, explaining how Desdemona had fallen in love with him.

"She loved me for the dangers I had passed. And I loved her that she did pity them."

"What?"

Had she said that out loud? She felt her cheeks burning. "Nothing, just thinking."

"About what?"

"About Shakespeare, if you must know." And she wasn't saying any more than that. Wasn't going to tell him she was dreaming about love stories and wishing someone like her could experience romance, too, even if just for the duration of a winter storm.

Carlo looked at Fern's face, so pretty in the flickering firelight, and drew in his breath. He felt so drawn to her. On a physical level, definitely. Behind those glasses, her eyes were huge. Her hair shone as glossy as polished mahogany around her shoulders, and her petite figure was the perfect slender hourglass. Half the town's library patrons probably came in just to get a glimpse of her.

But her appeal went beyond the physical. She'd drawn him out into talking about things he never talked about, and she really listened, unlike a lot of people for whom conversation

was an opportunity to talk about their own issues and lives. She seemed really interested,
and she'd made him think.

She was quite a woman, and with the way
she was looking at him right now, he was in
real danger of losing his heart. But the problem was, it was all going to blow up, and soon.
Once the plows came through and they all re-
joined the real world, it was just a matter of
days until the truth came out about him being
Mercedes's father.

Now he wished he'd told her right away.
What would have been the harm? He should
have announced his suspicions that first night,
despite being sick as a dog and dizzy and un-
sure.

Yeah, he'd had his reasons. He hadn't wanted
her to get mad and kick him out and then be
stuck here alone. Before that, he remembered,
he'd wanted to investigate the situation and
pick up clues about how to approach getting
custody of Mercedes.

He'd never dreamed he'd get to feel so close
to her. That he'd care what she thought of him,
or that it would matter if she hated him.

Because she would hate him, he was pretty
sure of that. No matter how he tried to explain
it, the reality was that he'd withheld the truth.
And Fern, who was stubborn and upright and

moral in addition to being cute and a very good mother, wouldn't stand for that.

So he needed to do everything he could now to convince her he was a good guy. And although he really wanted to drag her into his arms and kiss the shadows away from her eyes, he needed to resist the temptation of those full, pretty lips.

He sat up and moved a little back and rubbed his hands together. "Enough about me. What about you, Fern? Don't you feel called to what you do?"

She cocked her head to one side. "I'm not sure."

"Being a librarian is doing good in the world, right? And if the Rescue River library is anything like it used to be, it does a lot for the poorer people in the community."

"Yes, I remember you said you used to take your sister there."

He held up a hand. "Stop trying to turn the tables. I want to hear about you, not talk more about myself."

She stuck out her lower lip in an unconsciously pretty pout. "I don't like talking about myself."

"Talk about the library, then. Do you still have programs for the poor and rural kids?"

She hesitated, then nodded. "Yes. We just

started a new one, in fact. Some of the migrant kids can't get library cards because they don't have a permanent address. So we started the friendly sponsor program. People in the community can offer their address to a migrant family, sort of guaranteeing that the books will come back. It ends up building some nice connections, in addition to making sure the kids can have plenty of books to read."

"Folks will do that?"

"The response has been amazing." In the dim light, her eyes glowed. "We thought we'd have a waiting list for the migrant kids, but instead, we have a waiting list of families wanting to sponsor them. I love Rescue River."

"Pretty impressive," he said. "And that was probably all your idea."

She looked down, then met his eyes, a smile tugging at the corners of her mouth. "Yeah. It was."

"And you don't think God has anything to do with your being in Rescue River and working at the library?"

Her brow wrinkled as she stared into the fire. "I don't know, maybe He does. I like my job and I've been able to help with some good things."

He noticed her modesty, her humility, and liked it. "But…"

"But what I really want to do is write and illustrate children's books. I could reach even more people that way. And it's as if there's something tugging at me all the time, pulling me into myself, into my...my dreamworld. I have so many ideas I want to share."

"Now that sounds like God."

"Is it? I can't tell. I feel selfish for even wanting to write."

"Selfish?" It was the last word he'd associate with someone who'd just taken in her friend's kid to raise. "How come?"

"Because it's so much fun!" She leaned back and looked up at the ceiling. "I have to kind of steel myself to go to work at the library every day, because it means so much time interacting with people. I'm an introvert, and it tires me out."

"I can relate," he said. "I need time to recharge myself."

"But when I'm writing and illustrating my children's books, I feel as if I could work all through the night and never stop. I have endless energy for it."

"And your work in the library has helped you, I'm sure. But maybe God's telling you it's time to go in a different direction."

Her eyes widened as she looked up at him. "Do you think so?"

His breath caught. Something about this pretty, passionate woman confiding in him and asking his advice took him to a place he'd never gone before. "Yeah," he said, reaching out to touch her chin with one finger. "Yeah, I think so."

Her eyes went wide and conscious then, and her tongue flicked across her lips. Sudden awareness of him as a man, he could guess that much, and he didn't know what to do about it.

Back in his previous life, he'd have known exactly what to do. With his wife, they'd been on the same page. Marriage had been more of an impulse than a true commitment.

He hadn't understood true commitment back then, and his actions had shown it. His choice of a wife had shown it.

But now it was different. He'd found Christ and realized the error of his ways. He'd learned what God wanted for a man and a woman, and it wasn't a one-night stand or even a short, intense relationship.

It was for life.

And he wasn't good for life. Not now, maybe not ever. He was still feeling his way with God, trying to understand where his work was supposed to go and who was supposed to be a part of it. So far, the only message he'd gotten clearly was that he needed to try to take care of his daughter.

Which he'd assumed would mean sweeping her away from an unsuitable and neglectful foster family and raising her himself.

He hadn't guessed he'd end up half falling in love with the wonderful woman who was already doing a pretty fine job raising his daughter.

He couldn't help it; he leaned in closer. Those full lips were so pretty and her eyes soft and questioning. He reached out and ran a hand along her hair, and it was just as soft and silky as it looked.

She opened her mouth and started to speak, then closed it.

He let his fingers tangle in her hair, just a little. "Is this okay?"

She bit her lip. "I…I don't know."

"How come?" She was as jumpy and nervous as a fawn and he needed to tread carefully here. His hormones were leading, for sure, but he needed to follow his heart and soul, as well.

She shook her head rapidly and looked away. "I just don't do this kind of thing," she said to the wall, her voice so soft he could barely hear it.

"Because…because why?"

She shook her head hard again and looked down. Were those tears in her eyes?

"Hey," he said, "we're not doing any particular kind of thing right now, okay? No need to be worried."

Her face went pink. "I didn't mean...I didn't expect you to..." She met his eyes, her face miserable. "I'm not the kind of woman men make passes at. Especially men like you."

He felt his eyebrows lift almost into his hairline. "That's hard to believe."

"No, it's true," she said. "I don't really date."

"Do you...have some kind of belief against it?" He knew she was a Christian, a fairly new one, and sometimes people put tight limits on themselves as new Christians. Though he couldn't imagine that Fern needed them. She seemed like such a balanced, thinking woman.

"No. I just don't get asked out."

"You're kidding."

"Not kidding." She tossed her hair out of her eyes and looked at him with a touch of defiance. "Guys just don't see me that way."

"You sure you're not putting up some kind of vibe against being approached?"

She cocked her head, then nodded decisively. "That, too."

"You're not putting out that vibe with me."

He let his hand curl into her hair again, and a whiff of flowery shampoo floated his way.

Lord, help! He wasn't going to be able to stop if he started kissing her.

"I'm not putting out that vibe because...I'm drawn to you." Her words were so quiet that Carlo had to lean in to hear them.

He shut his eyes, still holding on to her. *Lord, what do I do now?*

But he already knew the answer: back off. Fern was an amazing woman, one of a kind, and she deserved much better than someone as damaged and bad at relationships as he was. Someone who was, even now, withholding the truth from her. She deserved a real chance at love.

He slid his hand out of her hair reluctantly, and put it on her shoulder. There, that was good. That was friendly and impersonal. "We're both vulnerable. It's been a long couple of days." He swallowed hard and let his hand drop. Made himself lean back away from her.

Her eyes widened with an expression of utter betrayal. "You made me tell you I'm attracted and then... Really, Carlo?"

"I'm sorry." His body was still at a fever pitch and he'd used up every ounce of his store of human kindness and patience and self-control. "I just don't think it's a good idea."

"You've got that right." She scrambled to her feet and spun around. "I can trust you to watch the fire, at least?" Her cheeks held high spots of color and her voice sounded shaky.

"Um, sure." Clearly, he'd done something wrong. He'd been trying to do the right thing, and he'd screwed up. At least with her, but maybe not with God, because backing off from romance, given the major secret he was keeping, was definitely the right thing to do.

But keeping his emotional distance wasn't easy, and he needed physical distance to do it. "I'll handle the fire," he said more gruffly than he'd intended. "Go on up to bed."

Chapter Eight

"Mama Fern, Mama Fern, there's trucks outside! And it's sunshining!" Forty pounds of excited four-year-old landed on Fern's stomach.

Fern squeezed her eyes against the bright light and wrapped her arms around Mercedes, turning on her side to snuggle the child close. "You're *my* sunshine, sweets."

But inside, she felt as if one of those snowplows—which she could now hear scraping and grinding gears out on the road—had run right over her.

After Carlo's abrupt rejection, she'd tossed and turned much of the night. She'd replayed it over and over in her mind: the way he'd gotten her talking, the things he'd shared, how close she'd felt to him, how comfortable. Had that been false?

She'd actually told him she was attracted to

him. Hot embarrassment flooded her chest and neck and face even now.

"Let's go tell Mr. Carlo!" Mercedes wiggled in her arms and, when Fern let her go, bounced upright.

Fern couldn't face him, not yet. "Mama needs to shower and get dressed. You can go tell him."

"Okay!" The child jumped down to the floor and ran out, yelling, "Mr. Carlo! Mr. Carlo! There's trucks!"

It was just another stab, how quickly Mercedes had gotten attached to Carlo. She'd expect them to stay friends, would want to see him.

Fern drew in deep breaths, a calming strategy she'd learned from a social worker way back when she was a kid and something awful happened. *Just get through the next hour, the next week.* Pretty soon the snowplows would break through, and they wouldn't have to see each other every hour of every day.

After that, Angelica would come home and Fern's vacation would be over. She could go back to her small life in her little house down the street from the library. She could focus on Mercedes and her job and her children's books. No more pretending that she could make it in the normal adult world of happy, promising relationships.

She wrapped her arms around her hollow-feeling stomach and trudged to the bathroom, but even a long, hot shower didn't lift her spirits.

Breakfast felt strained, even punctuated by Mercedes's happy talk and the sound of the plows and a few other vehicles driving by outside. Apparently, the county had gotten the road clear. Fern broke her own rule about keeping her phone away from the table and texted John Allen Bunting, who plowed the farm roads and driveways. From him she learned it would be another hour or two before they were fully out.

Before Carlo could leave.

Oh, she wanted him gone. It hurt to look at him. Because like a fool, she'd gone further than getting attracted to him. Somewhere during the past three days of snowbound privacy, she'd lost a piece of her heart to the man.

To avoid him, she washed the breakfast dishes by hand, looking out the window into the blindingly sunny, snowy world. When would John Allen and his plow come? When could she escape this torture of being stuck in the house with the man who'd broken through the walls around her heart just so he could crush it?

"Hey." He touched her shoulder, a tiny taste of the fruit forbidden to her. "You okay?"

"Fine." That came out harsh, so she tossed him a fake smile to soften it. Trying to be subtle, she eased her shoulder out from under his hand.

Instead of letting her go, he clamped his hand down tighter. "No. Uh-uh. What's wrong?"

"Nothing's wrong!" She spun hard away from his hand and from that patient, patronizing tone in his voice. As if she were Mercedes's age. *Come on, John Allen, get your plow out here.*

He took a step backward, hands up. "Whoa. What's going on? Are you upset about last night?"

"Just...leave...me...alone." She ground out the words through clenched teeth and turned back to the sink, plunging her hands into the warm, soapy water.

He started to walk away and then turned back. "No. No, I'm not willing to leave it like that. The plows will be here soon and I—"

"Let's hope," she interrupted and then stared down at the suds, taking deep breaths. "Where's Mercedes? Would you mind keeping her busy for a little while?"

"She's playing with her dolls. She's fine."

And indeed Fern could hear the chirp of Mercedes's pretend voices from the living room.

Get a grip on yourself. At all costs, she had to avoid letting him see into her soul again. Had to protect herself from more of the hurt that had kept her awake all night. Staying inside herself was safer.

No fighting. That was too passionate. "Did you sleep okay?" she asked brightly, grabbing a cup and plunging it into the soapy water.

"Fern. That's already clean." He reached in and pulled the cup away from her, and their hands touched in the soapy water, slippery and warm.

Something like electricity shot through Fern's hand, up her arm and straight to her heart. Carlo's spicy aftershave tickled her nose.

He sucked in his breath. "Talk to me. What's going on?"

She pulled away from all the feelings and shook her head.

"Last night, I felt we were getting so close. And now you've shut me off."

"You shut *me* off!" The words burst from her and she clenched her jaw to keep from saying more.

He was still standing so close, half behind her, and he leaned sideways to see her face.

She tucked her head down, but heard his soft exclamation.

He moved away and the space where he'd been felt cold, as cold as the icicles that hung outside the windows, sparkling and dripping in the sunlight.

And then he was back with a dish towel. He took her ever so gently by the elbows and pulled her away from the sink. Turned her around as if she were a child—and she was, size-wise, compared to him—and dried her hands. "Come on," he said, pulling her toward the table. "Sit down. I have to talk to you."

She didn't want this, didn't want to get into some long discussion of her own inadequacies. Clearly, he felt bad. "It's…I have a lot to do before the plows come. And you do, too. You have to get your stuff together."

A muscle twitched in his jaw. "I know, but I think we've got ten minutes for a conversation, right?"

She looked at the clock on the wall, an absurd teakettle with a face. "I'm not going to get out of this, am I?"

"No, Fern. We need to talk."

She jerked out a kitchen chair and sat down. "So talk." She was behaving like a sulky teenager, but it was better than being a lovesick idiot.

He raised an eyebrow and spun another chair

around so he could straddle it, leaning his arms on the chair's back as he faced her. "I'm sorry I let those romantic feelings build last night. Is that what you're upset about?"

Let him think so. Let him think the mousy librarian was offended by his miserable joke of a pass. "Sure."

"I...I try to live a good Christian life, but of course I fail a lot, like every other human. You're pretty and real and warm. I got attracted to you, and I let it show."

She nodded without looking at him. He hadn't gotten all that attracted, apparently; he hadn't even kissed her.

He ran a hand over his hair. "In that kind of situation, when I'm feeling stressed or pressured or tempted, I try to grab on to God. He helps me, but it's not always pretty."

"Oh, yeah, I'm sure you've been in that kind of situation a lot."

He cocked his head to one side. "Lots of emergencies, yeah."

"Lots of women, too, I'm sure." Why was she talking about this? She sounded like a jealous fool.

He shook his head slowly. "Not so many women. I was thinking more of other kinds of danger. You get good at those battlefield prayers." He studied her. "No, I haven't felt like that about a woman in… Well, ever."

"Right."

"It's true. There's a, I don't know, some kind of spiritual dimension to what I—"

"Look, why are you trying to flatter me? It was crystal clear that you didn't want to kiss me, and I understand that. There's no need to pretend otherwise. In fact, it's kind of insulting."

He reached out and put a hand on either side of her face, forcing her to look at him. "I'm not lying. I really wanted to kiss you."

Was it true? Could it be true?

"I wish…" He broke off, shaking his head.

"What?" He looked so concerned and so vulnerable that her hurt feelings floated away. Borne by that line he'd started to say… What was it? That there was a spiritual dimension to what he felt for her?

Could a librarian and a mercenary be soul mates?

He flashed a smile that just about devastated her. "I wish we could stay here awhile longer. Just the three of us."

And then he unstraddled the chair, stood and pulled her into a hug.

She wanted to protest. Needed to protest, needed to stop this. But the truth was his touch felt wonderful. The careful and respectful way he cradled her against his chest made her feel safe, safe in a way she never had felt before in her life.

She remembered seeing other kids held by their parents like this, cuddled lovingly but with nothing malicious in the intention, no worries that things were going to go in a wrong direction. The only times she'd been hugged or held, that she could remember anyway, there'd been an accompanying smell of liquor on the breath and hands where they shouldn't have been. Those times, she'd struggled to get away.

And she'd learned to cross her arms and look away and keep her distance. She'd learned that getting close only led to something that felt ugly, a mockery of closeness. With a flash she understood why nobody ever asked her out: she'd learned to put out the "go away" signal, and she'd forgotten to let go of it after she was an adult and safe.

Only Carlo had cared enough to push past that barrier, and he'd done it last night. He'd gotten her to talk, and touch, and feel. He'd told her of his admiration for her and he'd listened closely to how she felt.

And when the time came for them to make a decision about where to go next, he'd backed off respectfully, choosing the wiser route for both of them.

Fern was an independent woman and she never, ever relied on anyone except herself. But maybe, just maybe, Carlo was someone else she could rely on a little bit.

He brushed back her hair and touched the corner of her mouth and looked into her eyes without smiling. "I still want to kiss you."

From a place inside her that she hadn't known existed came a half smile and a warm feeling. "Why don't you do it, then?" The words came out in a husky whisper, not sounding like a prim, shy librarian at all.

His eyes went dark and he looked at her lips, then back at her eyes. "You're sure?"

She only nodded, staring at him.

"Whatever else happens," he said, "whatever you see or hear or think in the future, just remember one thing."

"What's that?" Her voice came out a breathy whisper and she was warm, so warm. She leaned toward him, her tongue wetting her dry lips. She'd never kissed anyone before, not except for a quick peck at the end of a bad date, but for some reason she had no fear at all. She knew Carlo could guide her through this.

She let her hand tighten on his arm, feeling

the muscle bulge beneath his thermal shirt, and drew in her breath with a gasp.

"I want you to remember, this is what's real." He touched her cheek with the tenderness she'd longed for her whole life.

And then he proceeded to kiss her thoroughly.

Now, why had he done that? As soon as Fern got up and walked wobbly across the room, leaned back against the counter and stared at him, hand to her mouth, Carlo started yelling at himself inside his head.

You're an idiot!

She's gonna be even more upset when she finds out the truth!

Should have stuck with the program from last night!

But kissing her had felt so very good. So perfectly *right*, and that was something he'd never experienced before. Kissing her, and not just that, but being here with her, felt like coming home. To a home he'd never had.

He was feeling an urge to pull Fern and Mercedes to him and never let go, to stay on a snowy farm with them forever.

And to do that, he needed to tell her the truth before the plows broke through. The idea of letting her know that he was almost for sure Mercedes's father made him break out sweating.

"We need to talk," he said before he could chicken out. "There's something I—"

"Let's play a game!" Mercedes came racing in, her hair a messy tangle of curls, still in her princess nightgown. She flung herself against Fern, looking up. "Please?"

So adorable, and Carlo felt a surge of love for her that was qualitatively different from anything he'd ever felt in his life. He'd lived to protect kids—that was half of what he'd been doing, fighting in Central America—but his own child multiplied anything he'd ever felt before by a number too big to name.

Even more important that he tell Fern, so that the two of them could work it out and figure it out, could do this right, in a way that made it good for Mercedes. "We'll play in a minute, honey," he said as Fern scooped the child up. "I have to talk to Mama Fern first."

Fern snuggled her face into Mercedes's hair and then cut her eyes at him. "But sometimes Mama Fern doesn't like to talk. Right, Mercedes?"

"That's right," Mercedes explained to Carlo, her face serious. "Sometimes Mama Fern's ears hurt from listening and her mouth hurts from talking, and we have to be quiet."

Fern's cheeks went the most perfect shade of pink. "And that's because..." she prompted.

"It's not anything bad about you," Mercedes said, reaching out to pat Carlo's arm reassuringly. "It's just the way Mama is made."

Carlo's heart expanded enough to hold a little more love. God bless a woman who could explain instead of yelling or shutting down, who could make a talkative little girl feel supportive and understanding about her mama's need for quiet time.

Fern was an amazing mother. And an amazing woman. And he really, really needed to find a way to tell her the truth.

"What game should we play, sweets?" she asked.

"I'll go get one of Xavier's!" Mercedes ran into the living room. He heard cupboard doors flung open, boxes rattling as they crashed to the ground. "Sorry," Mercedes sang as she banged the boxes around.

"Fern—"

"Looks as if John Allen just started on the farm road," she said, flitting away from him, hurrying through the door and into the living room to peer out the picture window. "It'll be a while until he digs our vehicles out."

He followed. "But just real quick—"

"It's an introvert thing." She put a hand on her hip and mock glared up at him. "Don't you get it? I need time to process things before I can talk about them."

"Let's play this one!" Mercedes produced a game from the stack and hurried to the fire. "You come sit here," she ordered, tugging at Carlo until he caved in and sat where she was pointing. "And, Mama, you sit here."

She'd positioned the adults on either side of herself, and they formed a little semicircle facing the fire. Facing away from the window, from the outside world.

Carlo drew in a breath and tasted a mix of happiness and fear, more intense than anything he'd felt in the worst jungle firefight.

"Come on, let's play!"

Obviously, Fern wasn't going to let him have the conversation he needed to have right now. And obviously, they couldn't have that conversation in front of Mercedes. So he did what he'd done in battle: forced himself to stay in the moment.

You did that by focusing on sensations, not thoughts. So Carlo took deep breaths, catching the whiff of baby shampoo from Mercedes's hair and something muskier from Fern's. He looked at the colorful children's game and stretched out his hand to the warmth of the flickering fire. Felt the soft fur of the rug beneath them, their little island.

"Your turn!" Mercedes nudged him, and he tried to understand the game. "What do I do?" he asked.

Fern chuckled. "It's for ages three and up," she said, holding up the box lid to show him. "It's not that complicated."

"You have to take your guy through the maze without waking up the daddy," Mercedes explained. "If you land on the ones where you have to push the button, you might wake him up."

Carlo obediently rolled the dice and took a card.

When Mercedes was done with her turn and Fern was taking hers, Mercedes looked at him seriously. "I don't have this game at home," she explained, "because I don't have a daddy."

"Oh, really?" His heart thudded in a sick way.

"Xavier has a daddy," she said thoughtfully. "So he has this game about daddies."

"I see." He glanced over at Fern, feeling that his guilt was written all over his face. But she was checking her texts, not paying any attention to their conversation.

"Xavier *got* a daddy," Mercedes said, studying him. "He didn't have one, but then he got one."

Was this his cue to speak? He stared into

the brown eyes so like his little sister's. *Lord? A little help here?*

"Right, Mama?" Mercedes leaned against Fern.

"What, sweets?"

"Xavier didn't have a daddy, but he got one," Mercedes explained patiently. "Maybe he—" she pointed at Carlo "—maybe *he* could be my daddy."

Carlo's heart just about exploded out of his chest, worse than that time a land mine had gone off six paces away from him and his buddy.

And just like then, he had the urge to preserve the person at risk. Had to protect Mercedes from finding out wrong, had to keep Fern from saying something negative about Mercedes's absentee daddy that would come back to haunt him.

He opened his mouth and closed it again. What could he say? Where did he start?

"Every family is different, honey," Fern said, stroking Mercedes's hair. She didn't look at Carlo, and he saw that her cheeks were pink. "It's hard not to have a daddy sometimes, isn't it?"

"Yeah." Mercedes scrunched her nose. "It would be fun to have a real daddy to wake up for real, not just in a game. And for Donuts with Dad at school."

Relief flooded him, a cowardly relief as he realized the moment of absolutely having to tell Mercedes the truth was passing, thanks to Fern's tactful words.

Right behind the relief, the enormity of what he'd done by not being there crashed into Carlo all over again. Mercedes had been going through life without a dad. Seeing other kids whose dads were there for them and knowing she wasn't protected like that. Of thinking her daddy knew about her and didn't care enough to show up.

"I know. Donuts with Dad was hard." Fern side hugged Mercedes and nuzzled her hair. "I didn't look much like a dad, did I?"

The pressure on him averted, Carlo stared at Fern. "You went to her Donuts with Dad day?"

"Well, yeah. She didn't have anyone else."

"There weren't any other single moms there?"

"Tommy Tremain had his grandpa there, because his dad's in a war," Mercedes explained. "And Sierra doesn't have a daddy, but her uncle came, and he's a fireman. Chief…" She looked over at Fern for help.

"Chief Kenny. Kenny Snyder," she added for Carlo's benefit. "Most people around here have extended families who can step in and help at times like that," Fern explained to Carlo. "But I… Well, I don't. And Kath's family isn't anywhere nearby."

"So that left you." His heart hurt, a little bit for Fern and a lot for Mercedes. And for himself, because he'd have loved to be there, but he hadn't even known he'd had a child.

"Yeah, I was the only woman." Fern wrinkled her nose. "A bit awkward. I'm not too good at talking sports with the daddies, but I can eat doughnuts really well, huh?" She ruffled Mercedes's hair.

"And Sierra's uncle sat by you the whole time!" Mercedes proclaimed. She cocked her head to one side. "Maybe *he* could be my daddy. Then I'd have a fireman. A chief!"

"Um, no." Fern was blushing now, and she snuck a glance at Carlo through her hair.

Carlo guessed all the dads had liked having Fern there. Especially Kenny Snyder, whom Carlo had known as a kid. Somehow Fern had gotten the idea that she wasn't attractive, but that was a bunch of hooey. Even her shyness was just…cute. The men had probably fallen all over each other to make her feel comfortable.

And that was a picture he needed to get out of his head, because it made him want to storm in and claim her in front of the whole town.

As they turned their attention back to the game, Carlo studied Fern. In all that conversation about fathers—which sounded as though Fern and Mercedes had been over before—Fern hadn't said one negative word about Mercedes's missing biological dad. He was grateful for that. And he could see, too, that telling Mercedes the truth about his own identity as her father would have to be handled delicately. She was of an age where she was noticing things, noticing how she fit into the world and how her own family compared with others.

He needed to get Fern aside and tell her the truth about his connection to Mercedes, but it might not happen today. Even now he could hear the snowplows scraping on the road, bringing the outside world closer.

He looked at the two heads bent over the game. Both with shiny brown hair, lit by sun, they looked like mother and daughter.

They looked beautiful, and he wanted to wrap his arms around both of them and protect them from a world that was all too cold and dangerous.

Treasure this moment. Because everything was going to change all too soon.

Could they just have one more hot chocolate? One more laugh over a silly mistake Mercedes made in the game? One more shy exchange of glances in front of a roaring fire?

But now the scraping sound was right outside the door, as if someone was shoveling the sidewalk, and Bull started to bark while the mama dog, Brownie, gave a low-keyed woof, as well.

When the knock came, Mercedes jumped up while Fern held on to Bull. "Don't ever open the door without an adult to help you check who's there," Fern warned. "Could you get that?" she asked Carlo.

He strode to the door right behind Mercedes. "Lift me up," she ordered, and he swung her into his arms so she could look out the high windows on the door.

And who was he kidding? So he'd get another chance to hold his daughter.

He looked out, too, and saw a smiling, bundled-up stranger with a shovel in hand. Drew in a breath, took one glance back at their warm, private haven.

Then he opened the door with his daughter in his arms and a sense of impending doom.

Chapter Nine

As the door opened, Fern took one last look around the room where they'd spent much of the past three days. With game boxes scattered across the floor, it looked a little messy, but the fire and the lamp and the mugs they'd used for hot chocolate brought back memories already.

It had been an unforgettable bonding time for her and Mercedes. And Carlo had been a huge part of that. Unexpectedly, he'd woven his way into the world she was building with herself and her child…and she hadn't minded one bit.

"Hey, hey!" It was Kenny Snyder, the fire chief, coming inside, stomping the snow off his boots. He was a warm, caring man, a deacon at their church. And so big and blustery and loud that she always found him a bit overwhelming.

"Sierra!" Mercedes shouted, and Fern realized that Chief Kenny had his niece, just a little older than Mercedes, with him. "I built a snowman, did you see?"

"I did, too." Sierra surveyed the room and then looked up at her uncle, shrugging off her coat. "Can I play with Mercedes?"

"Sure. That's why I brought you." He bent down to help her take off her snowy boots, talking to Fern and Carlo at the same time. "Everyone from the congregation knew you were stranded out here and we were all concerned. Since I'm a deacon, I got elected to come and check on you. And since little miss here was driving her mom crazy at home, I decided to bring her along to see her friend Mercedes."

"That was nice of you," Fern said. "Come on in, Sierra. You can pet Bull, just be gentle. He's an older gentleman." She made sure the child knew how to interact with a dog and then loosened her grip on Bull, who proceeded to lick Sierra's hands.

Mercedes was still up in Carlo's arms, and Chief Kenny cocked his head to one side and looked at both of them, a puzzled expression on his face.

"This is Carlo Camden. Angelica's brother?" She hurried to introduce the two men as Mercedes struggled to get out of Carlo's arms. "He showed up unexpectedly to visit his sister just as the storm was started, so he's been here with us."

"We knew each other in school, but it's been a while." Carlo put Mercedes down and held out his hand to shake with Kenny, who was still studying him with some puzzlement. "We made it through the storm just fine. Fern and Mercedes were troupers, even when the power went out. But it'll be good to get some help with the dogs again."

As if on cue, Bull barked once and that roused Brownie and her puppy. Once little Sierra saw them, there was no question about where the girls would play. "Explain to Sierra how to be gentle with Spots," Fern called over the children's excited shrieks, knowing Mercedes would love to be the authority figure to the other girl.

Their little private world had been invaded, and Fern couldn't help regretting it. Spending time with Carlo had been surprisingly peaceful—well, mostly—but Chief Kenny and his niece were loud and energetic and it was already giving her a headache.

As was the fact that he kept staring at Carlo. What was that all about?

And then she realized that he was probably thinking they'd spent the nights together. Her face heated, not only because of the inference but because it had a tiny basis in truth. An attraction *had* grown between them, culminating in some romantic moments last night and a very sweet kiss this morning. One that had left her feeling full of promise.

Still, she needed to do damage control, because Chief Kenny was a big talker and knew everyone in town. "Um, Carlo, when you go out to your truck, I can help carry your stuff. From the TV room. Where you slept."

Carlo looked at her blankly. "Okay."

She shot him a "help me out here" look and went past the girls into the TV room, returning with a pile of blankets and pillows. "Carlo slept in there," she said pointedly to Chief Kenny.

"Oh!" Light dawned on the man's face. "Well, of course he did! It's great you had some help." He kept looking at Carlo. "I just can't shake this weird idea… Mercedes, honey, come over here a minute."

Always eager to please, Mercedes ran over.

"Stand right there."

"Uncle Kenny!" Sierra complained. "We want to play with the puppy."

Carlo rubbed the back of his neck. His face had gone pale and he opened his mouth as though he wanted to say something. But no words came out.

"Can I go back and play with Sierra now?" Mercedes asked politely, and Fern smiled at her daughter's good manners.

The chief nodded. "Sure, of course." After she was safely occupied with Sierra, over in the corner where the dogs were, he turned to Carlo again. "Mercedes looks exactly like you used to look as a kid," he said. "I just can't shake the idea that you're somehow related. You look as alike as father and daughter! Of course that couldn't be." He looked from Carlo to Mercedes and back again. "Could it?"

Fern looked at Carlo, waiting for him to laugh off the fire chief's odd notion.

But Carlo's face was still and sad and solid. "It's possible, but Mercedes doesn't know," he said quietly. He shot her a quick glance, then looked back at Kenny. "Neither does Fern. There are a lot of steps to take, so I'd prefer you keep that speculation to yourself."

Chief Kenny lifted his hands like stop signs. "Of course! Of course! Sorry." He went on talking while Fern's world whirled into a faster and faster rhythm until she thought she might pass out from the dizzy feelings.

Chief Kenny had asked if Carlo was Mercedes's father.

And rather than denying it, he'd said, "Mercedes doesn't know."

She reached for a chair arm and sank slowly onto the edge of the chair, because her legs felt so shaky. "You said Mercedes didn't know," she said to Carlo, her brow furrowing. "And that I didn't. Does that mean…you did?"

He squeezed his eyes shut for a moment and then came over to squat in front of her. Chief Kenny was still talking, backing away, going across the room to kneel down by the girls and the dogs.

"Fern…I—"

"You *did* know. Is it true? Are you Mercedes's father?"

"I—"

"Don't you dare lie to me." She kept her voice soft so Mercedes wouldn't hear, but the fury she felt had to be coming through. "Anymore. Don't lie anymore."

"Fern. When I got here, I was sick. Practically delirious. I had no idea of finding…of finding my daughter in this house. I came to see Angelica."

She couldn't even process his words, because the enormity of what she'd just learned was pressing down on her. *Carlo was Mercedes's father.*

If it was true, if he was Mercedes's father, then all his kindness was false. Mercedes's father had left her, abandoned her, left her to live with Kath when she was deep into drugs. He'd let Mercedes be neglected and scared and alone all those years, put her at risk.

"You're a big military hero, but you couldn't take care of your own child?" The words burst out of her.

He blinked and shook his head back and forth, slowly. "I didn't know about her, Fern. I didn't even know she existed until a few weeks ago."

"How can that be?" Her voice had a little hitch in it, and she took a couple of deep, gasping breaths to calm down. "How could you not know?"

"Kathy kicked me out and I went back to the jungle." His voice was patient, calm. Infuriatingly so.

"Doing your important missionary work?" He was still squatting in front of her chair, trapping her, and she couldn't bear it. She nudged at him with the side of her foot. "Could you… move?"

He shuffled over to the side, still on his knees and too close. "I wanted to try to work things out with her, Fern. That's why I came home, after I found the Lord."

She waved her hand. "You keep talking and talking. You're full of excuses. But a little girl has suffered. Your own child."

Suddenly, Mercedes was there, looking worried, putting a hand on each of them. "Stop fighting! Kind words and inside voices."

"Sorry, Mercy." She kept the words in a whisper to hide her near hysteria. And she looked: from Carlo to Mercedes, from Mercedes to Carlo.

How had she not noticed what Chief Kenny had seen instantly? What kind of idiot was she?

She drew in another breath and forced calm into her voice. "Run and play with Sierra, honey. Look, she's holding Spots!"

Mercedes turned. "No, not like that, two fingers!" she cried, and ran toward Sierra. Chief Kenny was beside her, looking their way with concern.

"Let's go in the kitchen and talk," Carlo suggested, and even though she didn't want to do anything the man said, she recognized that he was right. She wasn't going to get any less upset. And she didn't need Mercedes seeing that.

God had chosen *this* man to do missionary work? Really?

She got to her feet, shaking off Carlo's helpful touch at her elbow, and walked to the kitchen on stiff, old-lady legs. She felt as if she'd been hit by a sledgehammer. She felt as if she were going to die.

"Are you here to take her from me?" she demanded as soon as they were in the kitchen.

He pulled out a chair for her. "Fern, there's so much we need to talk through. And I can't tell you how sorry I am to upset you like this."

"You *are* here to take her away. You tricked me on purpose, to get her to like you, and it worked, and now you're going to take her away." At the idea of losing Mercedes, a huge dark gulf opened inside her. She wrapped her arms around herself and stared down at the floor, trying to hold herself together.

She'd tried so hard to give Mercedes everything she needed, and it had brought her so much joy to do it. And Mercedes was making progress, feeling more secure by the day. To change things now, to have her go live with her father...with Carlo... She lifted her eyes to look at him. "I'm not letting you have her."

"Look, Fern, I know you're angry. We can talk this through."

His kind, understanding tone lit a fire in her. *He* wasn't upset. *He* wasn't angry.

Because he was the one who had just calmly ruined her life and that of the little girl she loved.

"You can talk all you want." She stood up then, poked him in the chest. "You can tell me all your excuses. But here's what I know.

You've neglected this child for her whole life, the whole time she needed you, and now you've come in and messed her up again. She thinks you're just some nice man, and now she'll have to find out you're her father, and you were lying to her!"

The calm expression was gone from Carlo's face now. He'd gone white, and now he took a step back, his fists clenching at his sides.

"What?" she taunted. "Nothing to say now? Why don't you try sweet-talking me? It worked to distract me from the truth before."

"I've got plenty to say." His voice sounded stiff, guarded. "But I'd better not say it."

"Go ahead," she challenged. This anger felt way better than despair.

"Fern, you're not thinking of that little girl in there. You're thinking of yourself and your own hurt feelings."

She narrowed her eyes at him. "You have no idea what's going on in my head."

"All I know," he said, "is that Mercedes wants a daddy. And now that I know about her, I'm here to be one. I think you're mad because it interferes with your neat little plan to have complete control of her."

"Oh, that's nice." She put her hands on her hips. "Start accusing me, will you? Take the spotlight off yourself. Maybe I *am* mad that you lied to me. That you…that you kissed me, just to get close to me so you could take Mercedes!" Was that true? Had his advances toward her been just about trying to get his daughter back?

She'd thought it was weird that a big, handsome, charismatic man like him was attracted to a mousy little librarian like her, but somehow, this morning, he'd made it seem believable. She'd gotten all happy. She'd even started imagining a future with him. But it was a big lie. "I need a moment," she said, and went into the pantry and slammed the door behind her, taking deep, gulping breaths, trying to regain control. Because if she didn't, if she really let go, she might never pull herself together again.

As soon as Fern left the room, Carlo sank down at the kitchen table and let his head fall into his hands.

How had everything gone so terribly wrong?

The pain on Fern's face was the worst thing. He'd gotten past some of those walls she'd built around her heart, he'd started to connect with her and then he'd caused her pain. He'd never regain her trust.

And maybe he'd never be able to have access to his daughter.

Lord, help. It was his simplest prayer, the

one he used when he was too weary and dis-
couraged for words. The one he'd used in the
POW camp. The one he'd used when his best
buddy had died in his arms.

He counted on the fact that God could fill
in the blanks. But how God could help with or
fix this, he honestly didn't know.

Fern came out of the pantry, grabbed a paper
towel and blew her nose. Then she turned to
face him. "It's best that you go now." Her voice
was completely, dangerously calm.

But Carlo didn't want to go. Didn't want to
leave this place that had held such happiness,
however brief. "We need to set up a time to
talk, figure some things out," he said. "Obviously, this was a shock, and I'm sorry—"

"Stop. Now."

The abrupt words surprised him into silence.

"I don't want to meet with you. I don't ever
want to see you again. You betrayed me, which
I obviously don't like, but you also betrayed
Mercedes, and that's unforgivable."

The words dug at his shaky self-confidence.
She was right. What had he been thinking,
coming back here?

"What kind of person does that? What kind
of person are you?" She shook her head, raising
her hands like barriers. "Never mind. Just go."

Inside, the part of him that had been a bad

kid, the talk of the town for it, came kicking and screaming to life. The way that hurt boy had reacted followed close behind the feelings, but Carlo was older now, wiser, could stifle the automatic flash of defensive rage. "You're angry. With good reason. But we still have to talk."

"I'm not talking to you!" Her voice was loud, sharp and a little scratchy, as though she wasn't used to yelling. Well, of course she wasn't. Fern was a quiet librarian.

Except when she wasn't.

The door to the kitchen burst open. "Hey, did you get things worked out?" The fire chief, whom Carlo couldn't like, not when he'd accidentally shoved Carlo under a bus, sounded booming and jovial.

Fern swallowed, the muscles working in her neck, and her fingers gripping the countertop turned white. "Carlo had just decided to leave."

"Not exactly right," Carlo said. "You'd decided I should leave. Which I'll do, as soon as we set up another time to talk."

"Hey, hey, I feel responsible," Chief Kenny said. "I...I maybe shouldn't have said anything."

"You were right to speak up," Fern said, her voice dripping icicles. "Otherwise, I don't know when the truth would have come out."

"Hey." Chief Kenny came up and put an arm around Fern, who cringed a little. "I'd like to help."

"I'd like some time alone," she said firmly.

The man looked startled, then nodded. "Yes, of course, I understand. Would you like someone from the congregation come to visit you? Maybe a woman."

"Who'd tell the world our troubles? I don't think so."

He patted her shoulder. "Not everyone's a gossip. I'll see if Lou Ann Miller can come over here. Won't tell her anything except that you could use the company, and you can talk or not, as you like. Okay?"

Carlo saw Fern fight the urge to wither the jovial, clueless fire chief with a choice putdown, saw the muscles in her throat move as she swallowed. "All right," she said in a resigned voice.

"And as for you," Kenny said, turning to Carlo, "I'd be glad to get together, talk over old times. Do you have a church home?"

"Oh, he's super religious," Fern interjected sarcastically. "He's a missionary. A real hero!"

"Is that so?" Kenny smiled hesitantly. He seemed to realize he was out of his element.

"I've been working as a missionary, yes," Carlo said. "And I'd be happy to get together sometime, but right now we need to set up a joint appointment with the social worker. Daisy Hinton?"

"Fine," Fern said. "Now get out." She waved a hand at Carlo and then turned to the fire chief. "I mean him, not you. Although—"

"Mama!" Mercedes stepped through the doorway, eyes wide, one finger in her mouth. "Why did you tell Mr. Carlo to leave? Stop fighting!"

Fern squatted down and held out her arms, and the little girl ran to her. Fern hugged her tight, tears running down her face like a stream over stone.

After a minute, Mercedes struggled free. "You're crying, Mama," she said, reaching out to touch Fern's face. "What's the matter?"

"Nothing you need to worry about, sweets." Fern's voice broke on the pet name.

Mercedes turned to Carlo and put her hands on her hips. "Were you mean to Mama Fern?" she asked him reproachfully.

"Not on purpose, but yeah. I hurt her feelings." Carlo was starting to think it was definitely a good idea to leave now. He'd gotten what he needed, a plan to meet with Fern and the social worker. Now he needed to get out before he blurted the whole truth to a four-year-old.

The trouble was, if he left, he wasn't sure when he'd ever see his child again.

He squatted down to Mercedes's level. "I'm going to go," he said, his throat tight. "Give me a hug?"

"Don't you dare." Fern moved to put herself between Mercedes and him. "Mercedes, go in the other room."

Mercedes started to cry. "Mama, he just wants a hug!"

"He wants a lot more than that," she said, her voice low and furious. "But he's not going to get it."

"Come on, my man," Chief Kenny said, clapping an arm around his shoulders. "Probably best to leave."

Carlo could tell from the fire chief's watchful expression that the man thought he was going to do something dangerous. Carlo was the bad kid by reputation, and maybe that wasn't just in the past. No one trusted him, and why should they? He hadn't exactly earned anyone's trust.

Two hours later, Carlo had gotten a room at the cheap hotel at the edge of Rescue River and was kicking himself for not doing that in the first place. Better to have braved an accident than to have ruined everything with his daughter.

But the roads were closed. And they needed your help.

When he thought of Fern and Mercedes out there alone at the rescue, what it would have been like for them to take care of the dogs and deal with the electricity going out, he had to be glad he'd been there.

He should have told the truth as soon as he'd realized it, that was all. He'd been an idiot.

After an hour of beating himself up, he pulled himself together, as he'd done so many times before. He called the social worker, Daisy Hinton—Sam Hinton's little sister, whom he remembered vaguely from his school years, and had seen most recently at his sister's wedding—and made an appointment to see her the next Monday. And then he took a shower and shaved and put on clean clothes. He had to get out of his miserable state of mind so that he could function, could get on his game and figure out how to play this right.

Somehow he'd envisioned returning to Rescue River a little differently. He'd thought he would come stay with Angelica and Troy, get his feet under him and get their take on the situation. When he was ready, he'd go to work on getting his daughter back.

His illness and the snowstorm and Angelica's absence had wrecked his plans. Not to mention that he'd met a woman who'd softened his jaded heart, who touched him in a way no one ever had...and then hurt her terribly. Now he had total chaos on his hands.

He tried to pray, but his thoughts kept circling back to all the ways he'd screwed up. He kept picturing Fern's hurt eyes and Mercedes's worried expression. He had a whole weekend to get through before he could move on this and fix things, and if he spent it in this tiny motel room, he was going to be in no shape to stand up and fight for his child.

Air, he needed air. He pulled on the down coat he'd picked up at the discount store on the way into town and headed out on foot into the little town where he'd grown up.

It wasn't five minutes until he ran into someone who knew him.

"Well, as I live and breathe, it's Carlo Camden," said a woman with gray hair peeking out from a furry hat. She wore a fur coat that reached to the top of her boots and she walked with one of those rolling walkers.

He squinted at her. "Miss Minnie Falcon?" Automatically, he straightened his shoulders and stuck out a hand to his old Sunday-school teacher. "How are you, ma'am?"

"Doing well for eighty-nine. What are you doing back in town?"

Of course she'd ask that, and of course he didn't have a ready answer and couldn't find one, not in the sharp light of those piercing blue eyes.

"I'm, uh, just visiting." He stuck his hands into his pockets, feeling as if he were fourteen.

"Visiting whom?" Her eyes were sharp with curiosity.

Did he have to answer her out of respect for her age? "A few people," he said vaguely, and turned the tables. "How about you? Are you still living in the same big place on Maple Street?" He remembered being invited to Miss Minnie's home as a Sunday-school kid, dragging Angelica along because there was no one else to care for her, and being petrified with fear that she'd put a dirty hand on the wallpaper or break a china figurine. But to his surprise, tart Miss Minnie, who'd seemed ancient even back then, had been kind. She'd taken one look at the rapid pace with which Carlo and Angelica were eating her cookies and made them sit down in her kitchen for a full lunch—sandwiches and fruit and milk.

"I sold my home to Lacey Armstrong two years ago. She's making a guesthouse out of it, although why she would do that, I don't know.

She wants to redecorate it in all kinds of modern styles, make it artsy, whatever that means."

In his old teacher's voice Carlo heard sadness and loss. "Where are you living now?" he asked gently.

Her mouth twisted a little. "I'm in prison over at the Senior Towers. My nieces and nephews insisted."

"Accepting visitors?"

She looked surprised. "Why would you want to visit an old lady like me?"

"Because," he said, "I learned about missionaries in your Sunday-school class, and now I've become one. I remember how you made missionary life sound so exciting. Thought you might want to hear a bit about mine, see a few pictures."

"Are you trying to raise money?" she asked, her eyes narrowing.

He laughed outright. "No. I'm not sure what's next for me."

"All right, then. You come and see me, and we'll talk."

She turned toward the Chatterbox Café, and when Carlo saw the table of gray-haired ladies waving, he figured the place was aptly named. The story of his being back in town, a missionary and planning to visit her, would give his old teacher a little bit of news to share.

He continued on down the street with a marginally better attitude toward the town of his youth.

He passed the bar where his parents had spent a fair amount of time. He was familiar with the place, having gone in to find his folks multiple times, especially when they were neglecting Angelica. On occasional visits back to town, he'd stopped in and seen some of his old high school cronies. But he'd given up drinking, not liking what it did to him or to others.

Across the street was his brother-in-law's veterinarian's office, and he wondered who was staffing it while Troy was traveling. An answer came when a man in scrubs walked out, helping an older woman carry a large dog crate. It looked like Buck Armstrong, a guy Carlo vaguely remembered as being in Angelica's class at school. He stopped and watched the pair walking toward the lone SUV parked in front of the clinic as he remembered what Angelica had said about Buck's struggles with alcoholism.

Apparently, before Troy and Angelica had gotten back together, Buck had asked Angelica out and then showed up too drunk to drive. He was a veteran, so Angelica said, and as he watched the man hoist the crate into an SUV, speak briefly to the owner and then stride back into the vet clinic, Carlo figured he might like to get to know him. Nobody understood a vet like a vet, and if the guy was drying out, he might welcome a friend who didn't socialize exclusively at bars.

Up ahead was the church. Carlo noted it for future reference and then turned down Maple Avenue.

Inside a building that he remembered as a dress shop, he saw decorations and renovations going on for what looked like a restaurant. Past that, he could see the Senior Towers, so named because, at six stories, they were the tallest buildings in town. Just visible was Miss Minnie's massive old Victorian, which apparently was being renovated, as well. What must that be like, for the old woman to look out the windows of her Senior Towers apartment and watch the innards of her old home being ripped out?

Yes, he'd visit her soon.

He turned the corner and there was the library, a squat brick building that had been something of a haven for him and Angelica growing up. Fern's workplace now.

Fern. He drew in a breath and let it out in a sigh, wondering how she was doing, whether she and Mercedes were enjoying some solitude or had gotten out for shopping or visiting.

Funny how a few days together had let him in on their routine. It was late afternoon, so Fern was probably fixing dinner, letting Mercedes help her, talking to the child in her serious way about measurements and kitchen safety.

He missed them with an awful, achy, scraped-raw feeling. Before he could sink into more sadness, he hurried past the library and came upon the park.

Every kid in town was there, it seemed, sledding on the small hill, enjoying what was left of a Friday's daylight. Whoops and shouts came from bigger boys on saucer sleds. He looked more closely when he noticed that several kids were sliding on cardboard, just as he and Angelica had done. Worked almost as well as a sled, maybe a little more adventurous.

He walked closer and noticed a couple of parents watching the sledding hill, calling out cautions to their kids in Spanish. On impulse, he greeted them in their native tongue, asking about their kids. It turned into a conversation, and Carlo learned that they were new in town, living on the same so-called Rental Row where Carlo had lived as a kid. They were from Guatemala, where he'd spent some time, and they shared a few stories. By the time he left, he had an invitation to their home for enchiladas—real ones, not the taco-joint kind.

He headed back toward the motel in a thoughtful frame of mind. There'd been a time when he wanted to run as far as possible away from Rescue River. The place held too many bad memories.

What he hadn't counted on was that he himself had changed. He'd grown up. And the town was changing, too, getting some new business, opening to some new kinds of people. Given its background on the Underground Railroad, it had always been a little more diverse than the average midwestern farm town, but it looked as though that diversity was increasing. The family he'd just met had said there were a number of people from Mexico and Central America in their neighborhood.

All of a sudden, Rescue River didn't look half bad. The problem was that his own ineptness had probably ruined his chances of building a home here.

Chapter Ten

On Sunday morning, Fern was dishing scrambled eggs onto Mercedes's plate when the farmhouse doorbell rang.

Her whole body tensed. Was he back?

Friday had been a rough day, with her own emotions so raw and Mercedes upset about how she'd kicked Carlo out. Yesterday, she'd managed to cocoon with Mercedes all day, reading stories, watching movies and playing in the snowy yard. Through it all, she'd tried to convey all the love and caring she felt for the little girl, sick at heart that their time together might come to an end soon.

She just hadn't wanted to face the world, not with her own humiliation about Carlo's betrayal so raw, and her fears about losing Mercedes so intense. But now Mercedes scooted out of her chair and ran to the door, clearly joyous about company.

"Wait, don't open it without Mama," she called, setting the egg pan down on the stove and hurrying after Mercedes. For all she knew, Carlo could have come to sweep the child away, legally or not.

He wouldn't do that, said a voice inside her. The voice that knew Carlo as an honorable, even heroic man.

You don't know him as well as you thought you did, said a rival voice. *He might*.

But when she opened the door, slender, silver-haired Lou Ann Miller stood there with a napkin-covered basket in hand. "Hello! I tried to call but couldn't get through."

"Spotty reception," Fern apologized. No need to mention she'd turned her phone off.

"Anyway, I made way too many of these rolls, and I wanted to share them with you and Mercedes. You like cinnamon rolls, honey?"

Mercedes squealed. "Mommy used to cook them. She let me pop the can and it made a bang!"

Lou Ann chuckled. "These are made the old-fashioned way, but they'll be almost as good as the canned ones. May I come in a minute, Fern?"

At that, Fern realized then that she was keeping a seventysomething woman on the porch in the cold. "Of course! We were just sitting down to breakfast. Would…would you like to join us?"

"Now, that's an offer I can't refuse," Lou Ann said. She handed her big puffy coat to Mercedes. "You find a place to put that, dear. Maybe right over there on the banister. No need to hang it up."

As she led the well-dressed woman toward the kitchen, Fern resigned herself to a lecture, probably an effort to get her to attend church. After all, it was Sunday morning, and only nine o'clock. There was plenty of time to get there for the ten-thirty service.

Normally, she would go. She'd been extra meticulous about churchgoing since she had Mercedes to care for, a young soul to raise up right. Today, though, she felt hopeless about that and unable to face the friendly, curious, small-town congregation.

"What a good breakfast you cook for that child," Lou Ann said as they approached the table, and the older woman's approval warmed her. She was glad she'd fixed a big pan of eggs, plenty to share.

She finished dishing them up, took the plastic wrap off the fruit she'd cut up earlier and whisked away the loaf of raisin bread, replacing it with Lou Ann's rolls. They all sat down, and Mercedes reached her hands out trustingly. "Can we sing my prayer, Mama Fern?"

"Of course." But Fern's own voice broke a little as Mercedes belted out the preschool blessing, backed by Lou Ann's deep alto. How long until she lost custody of Mercedes?

"You know the prayer!" Mercedes said to Lou Ann as she grabbed for a cinnamon roll.

Lou Ann helped her to serve herself. "Of course. I learned it from Xavier, right here in this kitchen."

So they chatted about Xavier and Angelica and Troy, how Lou Ann had helped Troy around the house when he'd broken his leg, how she'd watched them become a family. "There's something about this place," Lou Ann said, looking around the cheerful kitchen. "It just seems to lend itself to people coming together."

Fern kept her eyes on her plate. It hadn't worked in her case, though for a brief, unrealistic moment, she'd thought it had.

"Mr. Carlo stayed here with us during the blizzard," Mercedes announced. "And I asked if I could get him for a daddy, like Xavier got Mr. Troy, but..." She shook her head, her face worried. "Him and Mama Fern had a fight."

"Mercedes!" Fern looked quickly at Lou Ann, expecting harshness and judgment.

But the older woman just nodded and helped herself to more fruit without looking at Fern. "Sometimes that happens."

"Uh-huh." Mercedes seemed to take Lou Ann's calm reaction as evidence that nothing was wrong.

Fern got a tiny flash of the same feeling herself. Maybe this was just a fight. Maybe there was still a chance.

Mercedes lifted her hands in a comical, palms-up gesture. "Whatever."

Both women laughed, Fern blushing a little, and Lou Ann patted Mercedes's shoulder. "As far as having a daddy goes, any man would feel blessed to have you for his little girl."

The child's expression faltered. "I'm probably not gonna get one. Can I go watch TV?" Without waiting for an answer, she darted from the table and into the TV room.

"Mercedes!" Fern started to stand up.

Lou Ann touched her hand. "Let her go. You have to choose your battles with little ones, and I must have upset her with my comment. I'm sorry."

Fern sighed. "She's sensitive about her lack of a father, and I think her mom told her some negative things before she turned her life around."

"That's tough. Plus, she's recently lost her mother. And she may not feel quite secure with you. It's only been a few months, isn't that right?"

"Yes, and the adoption isn't finalized." Fern felt an uncharacteristic urge to pour her heart out to Lou Ann, but she stopped herself. "There's a lot of uncertainty. A lot to worry about."

"I'm sure." Lou Ann stood up and started carrying dishes to the counter before Fern could stop her. "You sit. I know this kitchen better than you do, and a single mom doesn't get many breaks."

The unexpected kindness warmed Fern, giving her a safe, cared-for feeling she wasn't used to. "But you're a guest."

"My offer comes with a price. I want you and Mercedes to come to church with me."

Of course. That was why she'd come. Fern had guessed as much. "Did Chief Kenny put you up to this?"

"Kenny told me you could use a visit," Lou Ann admitted. "It was my idea to do it Sunday morning. You could ride in to church with me."

"And be trapped into staying for the social hour, too?" Fern blurted out the words before she thought and then clapped her hand to her mouth. "I'm so sorry! It's a generous offer and I really appreciate it. I'm just…having some trouble right now, and I don't think I can face everyone."

"Then, drive yourself and sit in the back. You need the message," Lou Ann said bluntly. "And so does that little girl."

Mercedes came in then, carrying the puppy, with Brownie trailing close behind. Fern opened her mouth to scold Mercedes for picking up the puppy without an adult present, but she clamped her mouth shut. *Choose your battles*, Lou Ann had said, and she was right.

"Well, isn't that a little cutie!" Lou Ann bent over to pat the puppy's head.

Brownie let out a low growl.

"Brownie, it's okay." Fern moved to comfort the mama dog and make sure she didn't lunge at Lou Ann. "She was separated from her pup for a while, and she's protective."

"That's how mothers are," the older woman said comfortably before turning back to load dishes into the dishwasher.

Feeling a sudden rush of sympathy for Brownie, Fern knelt beside the big dog and wrapped an arm around her, rubbing her ears. Mercedes set the puppy down beside Brownie and they all laughed as its legs splayed out on the slippery floor. For the first time since Carlo had dropped his bombshell, the pressure in Fern's chest eased a little.

Lou Ann was kind. And she was also right. Both Fern and Mercedes needed to get out, and they needed a good dose of spiritual comfort. "I think we'll take your advice and go to church," she said to Lou Ann. "I'll drive so you don't have to come back out here, but thanks for the push. We needed it."

That was how Fern and Mercedes ended up sliding into the back row of the little white clapboard church a minute after the service started. Just hearing the praise music made Fern let out her tight-held breath in a sigh.

There was a force in the universe bigger than she was. There was a God who cared, not just about her, but about Mercedes. Which meant she could rest a little, could put at least some of the weight of the child's future into the Lord's capable hands.

Mercedes ran happily up to the front during the children's sermon and then went off to children's church. Fern breathed slowly in and out and watched the sunlight turn the stained-glass windows into jewels. The scripture passages and the sermon washed over her, providing a sense of comfort, a hint of peace…

at least until the pastor started talking forgiveness and reconciliation.

Hearing it in the abstract made excellent sense.

Thinking about actually doing it, especially where Carlo was concerned... That was another matter.

Oh, there was a part of her that wanted to forgive him. To tell him what he'd done was fine, to try to recapture that sweet, sweet hope that somehow her solitary life could expand into something bigger, that love could heal her lonely heart.

But that was wishful thinking.

After church she edged toward the door, hoping to slip down the back stairs to the children's wing, pick up Mercedes and escape. But everyone, it seemed, knew she and Mercedes had been stranded out at the dog rescue, and the kind expressions of concern trapped her.

And then she heard Mercedes's voice coming from the front of the sanctuary. "Mama Fern, Mama Fern! Look who found me!"

Carlo.

Heads turned at the sound of the happy, excited, little-girl voice, and everyone smiled and cooed at the sight of the handsome man carrying the adorable child.

Fern's own heart hitched, then pounded

hard. Carlo was amazing. Glorious. Protective. A hero.

Yeah, and how many of the friendly, admiring congregation were noticing what Chief Kenny had noticed, the strong familial resemblance between Carlo and Mercedes? What was Carlo thinking?

Fern marched over, took Mercedes from Carlo's arms and set the child down. "You do *not* have the right to pick her up from Sunday school," she whispered hotly.

Mercedes stuck her finger in her mouth, looking worried, and Fern's stomach lurched. She squatted down to comfort her, but just then Mercedes caught sight of one of her Sunday-school friends opening a sparkly pink purse a couple of pews down. "Can I go play with Addison?" she begged.

Addison was a godsend. "Sure," she said, standing up. As soon as Mercedes was out of earshot, she turned on Carlo, ignoring the way her heart raced just at his nearness. "Picking her up from Sunday school was totally out of line."

"I'm sorry. I was down there helping move some props for the puppet show and she saw me. The teacher let her come with me after I explained our connection."

Her eyebrows lifted practically into her hairline. "You explained your connection?"

"The blizzard," he said patiently. "Give me a little credit, Fern."

She couldn't match his calm tone, so she settled for keeping her voice low. "Chief Kenny recognized your relationship the moment he saw you with Mercedes. What makes you think everyone else in the church won't?"

"Would that be such a disaster? Everyone will know soon."

Fern looked over at Mercedes, now engaged in a game of pretend with Addison's plastic ponies. The church was emptying out. Fern leaned back against the side of a pew, frowning up at Carlo. "Yes, it would be a disaster! What if Mercedes finds out?"

He drew in a breath and let it out in a sigh. "I'd like to talk to you about how to tell her. I tried texting and calling, but I couldn't get through."

Yeah. That. "I did turn my phone off," she admitted.

"Hiding?"

"Would you blame me?"

He leaned toward her a little, and his hand lifted as if to touch her hair.

She sucked in a breath, shook her head.

His hand dropped. "Hiding is understandable. But, Fern, I want you to know I made an appointment with the social worker for Monday. It would be nice if you could be there. Maybe that's a way for us to talk calmly about this."

Fern felt as if the world was closing in on her way too quickly. She bit her lip and looked away.

"We can't delay on this," Carlo said. "Like it or not, it's a small, gossipy town. News travels fast. I'd like to figure out how to tell Mercedes, as well as how to proceed from here. Daisy agreed."

"You *told* Daisy?"

His brow wrinkled. "Of course I told her. She's the social worker. As soon as I got Kath's letter, I mailed her a copy and let her know I wanted to take care of Mercedes. When I talked to her yesterday, she was supportive."

Fern lifted her eyes to the church rafters, trying to breathe calmly. Daisy was supportive.

Fern was going to lose Mercedes.

"Oh, Fern!" A woman Fern had met a few times at the elementary school, whose pretty Asian features contrasted with her church-unconventional leather jacket and jeans, came up behind them. "Good, you're here. I wanted to suggest that you come ice-skating with the church group. It's a singles event, but kids are welcome, so you could bring Mercedes." She paused and then looked up at Carlo. "Hey… Carlo? You're Angelica's brother, right?"

"That's right," he said. "Susan. I remember you from my sister's wedding. Good to see you."

"You should come, too, if you're going to be in town," Susan said, and Fern felt a burn of jealousy so intense she had to put her hands behind her back to hide their clenching. Who did this woman think she was, horning in on Fern's man?

And where had *that* ridiculous thought come from?

"Think about it. Info's on the church website." Susan gave Fern another smile and then headed off toward another group of people talking.

Fern had to deal with this and she had to work with him and she had to quit acting as if she were the center of the universe. For Mercedes's sake, they had to work together. "All right," she said. "I'll come to meet with you and Daisy. But I warn you, I'm going to fight to keep custody of her with everything I have."

"Of course. You're a considerable adversary, and I do respect that." He turned abruptly and walked away.

A considerable adversary? Fern thought about the term and wondered. Was that what she wanted to be?

On Monday morning, Carlo arrived at Daisy Hinton's office half an hour early, hoping to catch the social worker before the official appointment and plead his case. He figured the deck was stacked against him, but he had to try everything he could to get at least some chance to be a father to Mercedes.

He entered the front door of the quaint brick building and passed a small, glassed-in playroom where a man sat cross-legged on the floor, playing trucks with a toddler.

Carlo clenched his jaw. That would be his fate if he didn't get Daisy on his side. Supervised visits in a little room.

He wanted so much more.

He wanted what they'd had during the storm. A cozy family life. But he'd ruined that possibility by his own stupid actions.

He reached Daisy's office. The door was open, so he tapped on the door frame as he looked in.

The short, well-rounded young woman with reddish curls tumbling down her back and rings on every finger bore a slight resemblance to the girl he'd seen around Rescue

River growing up, not that his ragtag family had run in the same circles as the wealthy Hintons. She'd been at Angelica's wedding, but then she'd been friendly and smiling. Today her expression was all business as she turned away from her computer. "Yes? Oh, hey. You must be Carlo." She frowned. "I thought our appointment was at ten."

"You're right. I came early, hoping to chat for a minute."

She gave one last longing look at the screen, cast a glance at the folders on her desk and then nodded reluctantly. Clearly, she was a busy woman.

Carlo waved a hand. "Go ahead, finish what you were doing. I'm sorry to intrude. Do you want me to wait outside?"

"No. Just give me a minute."

While she tapped on her keyboard, Carlo looked around the office, trying to get a bead on the woman who had control of his future and his happiness. A fountain bubbled in the corner, and paintings of large, bright flowers covered the walls. The couch and chairs and coffee table looked like somebody's living room—an artist's, maybe—and the subtle scent of vanilla added to the hominess. A big basket held a variety of children's toys. For Mercedes's sake, he was glad that if she'd had to spend time in a social worker's office, it was a cozy one.

"Okay, that's that." Daisy turned her chair to face him, and despite her colorful appearance, her level gaze told him she was the no-nonsense type.

He decided that total honesty was his best policy. "I think I really messed up by meeting Mercedes before I was supposed to. We got to know each other and got friendly, but she has no idea I'm her father."

"So you mentioned on the phone." Daisy fumbled through the stacks of file folders on her desk, finally coming up with one that, he figured, must be Mercedes's. "She's four, right?" She scanned the file with practiced eyes. "Four, going on five. So she's young enough not to do a lot of logical questioning. We might be okay, if you and Fern handle the telling with sensitivity."

"I screwed up with Fern, too, by not telling her the truth as soon as I suspected Mercedes might be my child. She's not happy with me now."

"Oh, really?" Daisy studied him, her gaze cool. "It definitely would have made more sense to build from a foundation of honesty. Why didn't you tell her?"

He stared at her wooden desk. "Aside from

the fact that I was half-delirious with dengue fever...I didn't know her at all. And I'm not a real trusting guy."

He suspected that would be the end of his credibility with Daisy, but he'd prayed about it and he was committed to being truthful now. He could only hope that would lead him back to the right path.

To his surprise, she sounded sympathetic. "I understand that. I'm friends with your sister after all, so I know how you guys grew up. But if you're not trusting, then why are you being up-front with me now?"

"Well..." Should he tell her he'd prayed about it?

"Is it to try to get me on your side before Fern comes in?"

"No!" He paused. *Tell the truth.* "Well, maybe a little. I just know Fern's dead set against me, and I really want the chance to parent Mercedes. To do a better job with her than my dad did with me and Angelica."

That admission seemed to soften Daisy. She nodded slowly. "I had a chance to verify the unusual circumstances between you and Mercedes's mom."

"Yeah?"

Daisy tapped her pen on the desk, looking out the window at the town's main street, and then seemed to reach a decision. "When she spoke to me, she'd told me Mercedes's dad didn't want any involvement. But that letter she sent you, the one you mailed to me, clarified that *she* was the one who'd hidden Mercedes's existence from you."

Carlo's heart jumped with hope. "So you don't hold me responsible for neglect?"

"No. And more important, the court won't, either, since we'll have her letter on record."

"Do I have a chance to get custody of Mercedes?" Even as he said it, an uncomfortable, guilty feeling rose in him.

The reason was Fern. Fern, and the important attachment she'd built with Mercedes. Fern, whose determination and beauty and strength had captivated him. He had opened his mouth to say so when Daisy raised a hand. "I'd like to hold off on discussing anything more until every participant of the meeting is here, for the sake of fairness."

"I wondered when that was going to occur to someone." The voice—Fern's voice—came from directly outside the office door.

Carlo jerked back to see Fern, hands on hips, jaw set.

"Fern! Come on in." A crease appeared between Daisy's eyebrows. "Did you hear what we were talking about?"

"I didn't mean to eavesdrop, but I'm upset you started the meeting without me." She cast a frown at Carlo.

She had a point, and guilt chomped at his gut.

Fern sat down in the chair Daisy was waving toward, her back straight, shoulders squared. "I think we should talk about what's best for Mercedes."

"Exactly," Daisy said. "Fern, I assume you now know that Carlo is very likely to be Mercedes's father. He's willing to take a paternity test—" She glanced over at Carlo. "Right?"

"Ready anytime."

"So we'll need to get Mercedes in for samples."

"Blood samples?" Fern squeaked.

"No. A simple cheek swab. We can have a tester come here."

Fern gave a short nod, but Carlo, watching her closely, saw her hands clench into fists, balling the material of her plain dark skirt.

He reached out to touch her arm, wanting to reassure her, but she jerked away. Daisy put her chin on her clasped hands, watching the two of them, obviously assessing.

Carlo felt that things were spinning out of control. "Look, I don't want to break the attachment Mercedes has with Fern. At the same time, as her father, I want to raise her."

"Looks as if you want two incompatible things," Fern said. Her voice was absolutely cool, absolutely level. Her hands clenched and unclenched on her skirt.

"Let's don't rush into anything until we have the results of the paternity test," Daisy advised. "I see that the two of you have some issues. We might need to go to court, but I'd like to work it out here if we could. Court battles are expensive and hard on kids."

Fern's face went pale. "I don't want to put Mercedes through that."

"Nor do I." Carlo leaned forward, elbows on knees. "Seems to me that we adults need to make sure we keep talking and try to figure it out. We all want what's best for Mercedes."

"I hope so," Fern murmured. Her voice was low, but it cut Carlo that she seemed to suspect he wasn't putting Mercedes first.

"It's always better for a child to have contact with her biological parents, as long as they're not abusive," Daisy said.

"I suppose," Fern said guardedly, and Carlo frowned, suddenly wondering about Fern's background. What had her family of origin been like? She'd mentioned something about foster care. If her own background was rough, that would be a factor in how she approached this situation. Just as his own background, having a mom and dad who couldn't parent well, had affected him.

"If the test comes back positive, which seems likely," Daisy said, "the first order of business will be to tell Mercedes about it. It's a small town and from what I understand, someone has already recognized some physical similarities."

"That's right," Carlo said. "It's urgent that we tell her rather than having someone ask Mercedes an awkward question. Can we talk about how to do that?"

Fern stared at him, and Carlo, knowing her as well as he'd come to, saw the moment when the walls went up inside her. She stood, knocking her leg against the coffee table and wincing, clenching her fists. "Look," she said, "it's obvious what's going to happen. You're her dad, and you're going to get custody of her. Excuse me if I need…a moment…to deal with that."

She spun away and ran from the room.

Carlo and Daisy stood at the same moment. "I'll go after her," Carlo said. "Please. Let me handle this." Though he had no idea how to make things right, his aching heart told him he had to try.

Chapter Eleven

Fern speed-walked past the Senior Towers and the library and the park and somehow ended up by the elementary school.

She stood outside the fence, looking in at a noisy crowd of children in winter coats and snow boots, black and brown and white kids all together, the sounds of English mingling with Spanish and what sounded like Vietnamese. She had to look pathetic, but she couldn't seem to move.

She loved Rescue River's little primary school, had been doing programs here regularly since she'd gotten the job at the library. After she'd taken Mercedes in, her visits gained new meaning. Soon, she'd be the mother of a child at this school.

Or so she'd thought. Not anymore.

Tears burned her eyes, blurring the lively

playground in front of her, and she dug in her purse for a tissue. Thankfully, as the mother of a four-year-old, she was well stocked. She blew her nose and wiped her eyes and took slow, deep breaths. She had to pull herself together, at least for long enough to get home to cry in privacy.

"Hey, you look pretty bad." The blunt voice belonged to Susan, the woman from her church who'd invited her to the singles event.

Oh, great. A teacher she knew *would* have to be on playground duty on the day Fern showed up crying.

"Anything I can do? Only catch is, I have to keep an eye on these little sweethearts, as well."

Fern shook her head, wiped her eyes and blew her nose. "Thanks. I…I'm having a few problems, that's all."

"Come on in. You can watch the kids with me and pull yourself together before everyone in Rescue River starts to gossip."

Fern didn't really want to socialize, but Susan had a point. "Okay."

"Gate's right over here." Susan walked with her on the other side of the fence until a couple of upset-sounding kid shouts distracted her. "Sorry, I've got to deal with this before it escalates. Hey, Mindy, what's wrong?" Susan headed toward the sliding board to mediate a very loud argument.

Fern was opening the gate herself when a large, male hand clapped down on her shoulder, sending what felt like tiny electrical shocks right to her heart. "There you are!"

Carlo.

Half inside the gate, she turned to face him. "What?"

He produced her coat and wrapped it around her shivering shoulders. "You left this at Daisy's office." Then he leaned closer. "You've been crying."

"Thank you, Captain Obvious," Susan said from behind Fern, and then stepped between her and Carlo. "What did you do to her?"

Carlo took a step back. "Hi, Susan. I'm afraid it's private."

"No problem, but we don't need any extra drama here at the school. Fern's welcome, she has her clearances, but you need to stay outside the fence."

The unfamiliar feeling of having another woman protect her gave Fern a tiny boost. She couldn't remember that last time that had happened. If ever. It helped that Susan showed no sign of romantic interest in Carlo.

A muscle in Carlo's jaw tightened. "Of course." He took a couple more steps back.

"Up to you," Susan said to Fern. "Come with me when I take the kids inside in, let's see..." She consulted her phone. "In three minutes. Or stay out with him. Either way, we need to close the gate. Mindy!" With the teacher's eyes in the back of her head, Susan must have noticed that a new circle of kids was gathering around the little girl who'd been involved in the fight a minute ago. "Be right back. I hope."

Carlo studied Fern through the fence. "Come walk with me. We need to talk."

She shook her head. "I can't. I...I just can't."

"Look, I know this is hard and awful. It is for me, too."

Fern opened her mouth to snap at him, but the defeated look in his eyes tugged at her heart. For the first time, she tried to look at the whole situation from his point of view.

He'd been rejected by his wife, not once, but twice. Then he'd gotten notice that she'd died and that he had a child, and he'd come rushing back to fulfill his duties, disregarding deathly illness to do so.

He'd met his daughter unprepared, had spent time getting close to her and now couldn't see her except under the care of a social worker.

The pain and conflict of all of it showed in his haunted eyes.

She lifted her hands, palms up. "I'm really

sorry, Carlo. I just don't see how one of us can win without the other one losing." And she couldn't sacrifice her stake in Mercy's future, because she knew she was an important part of the child's stability.

She put a hand up to the tall chain-link fence at the same time he did. They pressed their hands together, staring at each other, neither of them smiling. Fern's heart pounded out of control.

Finally, he spoke. "We need to figure out how to tell Mercedes the truth. That takes priority. After that…" He paused a moment, as if considering how to say something difficult.

"What?" Her voice came out as a feathery whisper she didn't recognize. "What after that?"

"After that," he said, looking hard into her eyes, "Maybe we can figure out this thing between us."

Hope and panic rose in her. Hope—and surprise, really—that he thought there was a thing between them. But panic, too, because it was all happening way too fast. "I don't feel as if I can figure anything out just now."

He pressed his hand against hers through the fence, curling large, blunt fingers though the chain links to clasp the tips of hers. "You're cold."

She couldn't look away. She'd been cold, too cold, for too long.

"You should go inside."

"I should." She licked suddenly dry lips.

One eyebrow lifted, quizzical.

How could she be feeling such wildly contradictory emotions toward this complicated, infuriating man?

Her confusion must have shown on her face, because he nodded once. "I'll be quick, then. After you left, Daisy told me option B. Which is having her tell Mercedes with the two of us, or just me, standing by."

"No!"

"Right. To me, that's not ideal. So let's have dinner tomorrow night and we'll talk it through, figure it out."

"Tomorrow?" She had no plans, but she needed time to pull herself together. Carlo's intensity scared her, plain and simple. "I can't find a sitter for Mercedes that fast."

"Then, Wednesday? We need to do this soon, Fern, before the cat gets out of the bag some other way."

It wasn't that she didn't want to see him. It was that she was desperate to see him. It was that his hand, gripping at hers, felt way too right for something that was totally wrong. "Okay, Wednesday," she said, then pushed off the fence, turned away from his too-perceptive eyes and hurried toward the school.

The sound of children yelling pulled her out of her own concerns. There was Mindy, the little girl who'd been fighting, struggling as Susan carried her inside. Other children were tugging at Susan's leg, trying to tell their side of the story. Fern looked around—surely there was another adult out here?—but the only aide was kneeling down beside a child who'd apparently fallen off the swings.

Fern quickened her step. "Hey," she said to the most persistent of the kids who was tugging at Susan. "Why don't you tell me what happened? And we'll see if we can find some answers in books next time I come for library reading time, okay?"

As she'd hoped, the offer of adult attention and a listening ear drew the clamoring kids away from Susan. She nodded sympathetically at the childhood tale of a push, the seizing of a ball and some name-calling, and promised to bring a book that told a similar story the next time. "Now, looks as if everyone's lining up to go inside," she said. "Show me how fast you can line up without talking."

As the kids lined up, Susan, still carrying the sobbing Mindy, cast her a grateful smile.

"I need to take her to the nurse," she told Fern. "Meet me in the teachers' lounge."

Because she didn't have anything else to do and no ideas about how to solve her problems, she did as Susan suggested. Every step through the school reminded her that she wouldn't have a child here after all. Carlo was trying to get along with her, doing better than she was. That would make him look wonderful to Daisy, the social worker, whom Fern had undoubtedly alienated by abruptly running away from her office.

She sank into a battered chair in the teachers' lounge and looked around, trying to keep from crying. The lounge clearly saw heavy use. Job-safety notices and motivational posters filled the pale green walls, and stacks of education-related magazines spilled off a table beside a worn vinyl couch. The sink was full of coffee cups and the window shade was tilted askew.

Fern grabbed a magazine and opened it, but tears kept leaking out of her eyes, blurring her vision. She grabbed a handful of tissues from the jumbo-size box on the desk, listening to the shouts of children and the remonstrating voices of adults, rising and falling as children headed to their classrooms.

Susan charged through the door, all energy, and perched on the edge of a chair beside Fern.

"Hey, you okay? I'm the only teacher with this planning time, so we should have the place to ourselves. Though no guarantees."

Fern wiped her eyes. "You probably have so much work to do."

"Nothing I don't want to procrastinate about," Susan said with a philosophical shrug. "Besides, I need to rest from carrying Mindy. She's not a small kid." She shook out her arms and rotated her shoulders, grimacing.

A bell sounded and the noise of children's voices faded. Class time again.

Fern wasn't quite ready to spill her secrets to a woman she didn't know all that well. "Yeah, what happened out there on the playground? Looked as if some kids have a history."

Susan nodded, "Yeah, you could say that. Mindy kind of has a double problem. You saw how she's missing a hand, right? But much worse than that, she also lost her mom a couple of years ago. She's one angry little girl, and she doesn't turn it inward."

"She fights?"

Susan nodded. "She isn't usually the instigator, but let anyone make a remark about her hand or her mom and she slugs them. No impulse control." Susan slapped a hand over her mouth. "Sorry. I shouldn't be running off at the mouth about a kid. Especially to a parent, or a future parent at least. Your daughter will be here next year, right?"

"If I get to keep her," Fern said. "It's…a question." Her throat closed on the last words and she stared down at her lap, trying to stop the tears.

"Wow, really? I'm so sorry, that's got to be hard." She paused. "Speaking of Mercedes, she probably has some issues similar to Mindy's. She just lost her mom as well, correct? And Dad's nowhere in the picture in her case. At least Mindy has her father."

"Well…" Fern met Susan's eyes. "Mercedes doesn't know her dad. But he *is* back in the picture."

Susan's eyes widened. "Wait a minute. Is Carlo Camden her dad?"

Fern looked away. "I… Look, Susan, he may be, but she doesn't know, so cone of silence, okay?"

"Totally!" Susan stared at her. "Oh, my gosh. Does Angelica know Carlo has a child?"

"If Carlo hasn't told her yet, I'm sure he will soon." She shook her head. "Even Carlo didn't know about Mercedes until a few weeks ago. Or so he says."

"Wow." Susan leaned back in her chair, staring at Fern. "So that's why he showed up in town. Every red-blooded woman in Rescue

River is aware of his presence, but I don't think anyone has guessed that much."

Fern looked sharply at Susan, noticing anew how beautiful she was. And she was so much more outgoing and friendly than Fern. A lively woman who could hold her own with Carlo, much better than Fern could herself. "So everyone's noticing Carlo?"

Susan lifted her hands, palms out. "Not me. I'm an anomaly. I'm not looking to date anyone."

"Oh? Why's that?" Susan would surely have her choice of men. Susan wouldn't have any problem getting what Fern herself, face it, wasn't ever going to have: a husband, a home, children.

Susan laughed. "I'm totally undomestic and I'm too sarcastic and blunt. Men are terrified of me. They want kinder, gentler ladies. Like you, Fern."

Fern shook her head. "I'm hardly a hit with guys."

"Really?" Susan looked skeptical, then shrugged. "Well, then that makes two of us. God didn't make everyone to be married. I'm finally getting comfortable with that notion, after a pretty unhappy experience being engaged."

Susan sounded vehement, and Fern looked at

her in surprise, startled out of her own troubles. "Wow, I never would have guessed. Especially since you run the singles group at church. I thought you were, well, looking."

"Anything but," Susan said, "but when you're single, friends are even more important. Which is why you should come ice-skating. We strong single women have to stick together."

Fern's tight muscles relaxed just a little. "Maybe I will."

"And listen," Susan said. "Just because Carlo showed up doesn't mean all hope is lost. I mean, didn't Mercedes's mom specifically want you for a guardian? That should carry some weight."

"Not much, from the look of things." Misery washed over Fern again.

Susan took her hand. "I'll pray for you, okay? You and Mercedes."

"Thanks." And as she got up to leave, she blinked wonderingly. She did feel the tiniest bit better after talking to Susan. And maybe, just maybe, she'd started to make a friend.

With a day to kill before he could see Fern and figure out how to tell Mercedes the truth, Carlo decided to stop at the Senior Towers on Tuesday morning. He'd promised Miss Minnie Falcon he'd come visit, but even more important, his grandfather lived there, and Carlo had avoided the man since arriving in town the week before. Okay, the blizzard was a decent excuse, but that had been over for several days and he still hadn't connected with Gramps.

They didn't always get along. Carlo had been harsh to the old man in his teenage years, insisting that he drop everything to take care of Angelica when their parents had dropped the ball. In turn, Gramps had been loudly critical of his own teenage misbehavior. When they saw each other, which was rare, they tended to grapple and circle like a couple of pit bulls.

Still, they were family.

As Carlo walked into the Senior Towers, he was surprised to see that the front lobby had plenty of people in it, enjoying the sun that poured through the windows. The repurposed apartment building had to be close to a hundred years old, but it felt a lot more homelike than more modern senior communities. The entryway had gleaming woodwork and high, old-fashioned tin ceilings. There were real plants in every nook and cranny, a colorful fish tank and lace curtains at the windows.

"There you are," Miss Minnie called, and extricated herself from a cluster of women to hobble toward a pair of chairs. "I've just been talking to the ladies about how you spent the weekend with that librarian who visits here, Fern Easton."

Whoa! She still had that Sunday-school teacher's voice that could silence a room. Time for damage control. "Yes," he said, giving Miss Minnie a kiss on the cheek and sitting down beside her. "I did end up staying out at my sister's place. When I got to town, I didn't know Angelica was away."

"You hadn't heard that she and that veterinarian husband went all the way to Europe to go to Disneyland?"

"Nope. But the roads were closed and the people Troy and Angelica had hired to care for the dogs couldn't get out there, so I was glad I could help Fern out."

"Mmm," Miss Minnie said, "I'm sure Fern was glad, too."

"Maybe," he said. "Although she was reluctant to have a stranger stay, the house is big enough that she was able to offer me a downstairs couch to sleep on." He wanted to be crystal clear that nothing untoward had gone on, knowing the likelihood that Miss Minnie would gossip. "Look," he said, "I brought some pictures from the missionary field for you to have. Thought you'd like to share your influence as a Sunday-school teacher."

The murmur of voices rose around them as people returned to their conversations. Good.

At the sight of the photos he'd brought, her eyes brightened with interest, and she asked a lot of questions about his missionary work. Carlo was just congratulating himself on how he'd turned the tables when Miss Minnie waved to a man who'd emerged from the small library adjacent to the lobby.

"Bob, come meet another veteran," Miss Minnie said. She turned to Carlo. "Bob Eakin was a glider man in World War Two."

Automatically, Carlo stood, greeting the leather-faced man and meeting his piercing blue eyes. "Thank you for your service."

"And you as well, young man."

"Carlo knows your favorite librarian," Miss Minnie said to the older man.

"You know our Fern?" The man looked him up and down and then gave a slow nod. "She'll be here today, matter of fact. Comes every Tuesday."

Carlo's heart thumped with a mixture of emotions. He wanted to see Fern, sure, but he also knew that she wouldn't be expecting him here today. Better to wait and not see her. That way he wouldn't nix his chances of getting on her good side tomorrow night. Someone like Fern didn't appreciate surprises.

"I thought Fern was on vacation," Miss Minnie said. "She's not been at the library, from what I heard."

"She'll be here anyway." Bob turned to Carlo and explained, "She stops in with new books. She knows we have a line of folks waiting to check them out."

"Leads a book discussion group for us ladies, too," Miss Minnie said.

"That one is smart. Reads everything in sight. Even knows a little military history." Bob nudged Carlo. "You could do worse. She took in that little gal when her friend passed on, no questions asked."

The last thing Carlo needed was a ninety-something matchmaker trying to push him and Fern together. She would hate that.

Which meant that Carlo needed to get on with visiting his grandfather and then get out of here. He said goodbye to Bob and Miss Minnie and, one short elevator ride later, was knocking on his grandfather's door.

"It's about time you got here." Gramps opened the door and then turned and headed back to his small living room.

Carlo followed him. "How you doing, Gramps?"

"I've been better. Heard you've been in town awhile. Glad you finally stopped by."

"I had some business to take care of, I've been sick and I got stranded in a blizzard. Is that enough excuses, or do you want more?"

"I heard about all that," Gramps said. "Ain't nothing to do around here except gossip, especially since your sister took her trip."

Hearing the loneliness behind his grandfather's words, Carlo felt his automatic defensiveness fade away. Gramps was feeling neglected and lacking his normal visits from Angelica, who'd always gotten along with the old man much better than Carlo had. "Sounds as if they're having fun over there," he said, keeping his tone mild.

"I don't see why anyone needs to go to Europe when we've got a perfectly good Disney World right here in the USA. Two, in fact."

Carlo chuckled. "There might be a few other appealing things about Paris."

"You're not staying for lunch, are you?"

Carlo hesitated.

"Don't bother if it's too much trouble."

"It's not trouble. It's just that…" He decided to be honest. If you couldn't tell the truth to family, who could you tell it to? "I'd like to stay, but I'm trying not to antagonize Fern. The librarian lady I met staying at Angelica's place? Heard she's coming to the Senior Towers today."

"About her." The old man's hand clamped down on Carlo's forearm. "Want to ask you something."

"Yeah?"

"Do I have a great-granddaughter I don't know about?"

The question hung in the air of the quiet apartment while Carlo's mind spun. He looked into his grandfather's eyes and realized he had the right to know.

He shifted in his chair until he was facing Gramps. "I think so. We went for a paternity test yesterday and should get the results back soon."

Gramps's eyes widened. "I've been hearing whispers, past couple of days, but I didn't believe it was true." His bushy eyebrows came together and he glared. "Why've you been so scarce, such that a stranger had to take in one of ours?"

"I just found out." He filled in his grandfather on Kath's letter and how he'd rushed home. "And the thing is, Mercedes—that's her name—doesn't know yet. Fern and I want to tell her ourselves, so please put a stop to any rumors you hear."

Gramps shook his head, his eyes on Carlo's. "Don't you remember how a small town works, boy? There's no stopping rumors. If you try, you only make 'em spread faster."

"What am I supposed to do, then?" He hadn't anticipated leaning on his grandfather when he came in here, but he was at the end of his rope. Fern didn't want anything to do with him, but his daughter stood to be hurt if they couldn't work out the adult problems.

"Back when I was young," Gramps said, "you'd do the right thing."

"What's that?"

Gramps looked at him as if he were a particularly dense specimen. "Marry her."

Carlo stared, then laughed. "You've missed a vital step. Fern isn't Mercedes's mother. She—"

"She is now," Gramps interrupted.

Carlo shook his head. "Kath was her mother, and I was married to Kath until she kicked me out. Fern is just…" He trailed off, because he knew that, in every way that mattered, Fern *was* Mercedes's mother now.

"Not trying to buck responsibility, are ya? That never was your way."

"No! I'm not…" He trailed off as he realized that he was trying to convince Gramps that he'd done his best, trying to gain absolution.

"Do you like her?"

"Who, Mercedes? Of course!"

"No, idiot. Fern. You like Fern?"

Carlo leaned away from the harsh voice and scrutinizing eyes, suddenly feeling about twelve. "I like her plenty. She's a great person."

"And you're at loose ends. Looking for a purpose, far as I can see. You've always wanted to help the underdog, probably because of how you grew up. Well, here's an underdog, and she just happens to be your daughter. How about marrying her mom?"

Carlo opened his mouth and then shut it as the possible solution coursed through his body and soul.

Marry Fern? Could he do it? Should he do it? Would she have him?

He focused on the probably negative answer to that question. "Not likely she'd have me if I asked."

Gramps crinkled his eyes shrewdly. "Scared?"

The word hung between them.

Slowly, Carlo nodded. "You know how I grew up. You know I haven't had a good example of marriage set before me, and I wasn't a good husband the first time. Why would it be any different with someone I'm marrying just for the sake of the child?" Although he knew in his heart that marrying Fern wouldn't be just about Mercedes.

"Ah, but—" Gramps wagged his finger at

Carlo. "Now you've got religion. With the Lord on your side, you can do a whole lot more than you can without Him."

Gramps got to his feet, leaning heavily on the arm of the chair but waving away Carlo's offer of support. "You better go on, now. Think about what I said. And make sure you tell that little one fast, because I got the feeling the rumors ain't gonna die down."

Carlo gave the old man an impulsive shoulder hug that had him waving Carlo away but looking just a little pleased. Carlo went down the elevator and headed toward the exit, his mind spinning. He needed some time to figure all this out. But he didn't have time, because the wagging tongues of Rescue River—not ill intentioned, but wagging nonetheless—were going to say something that would filter back to Mercedes. And he couldn't stand the thought of his daughter hurting that way.

She *was* his daughter, he was sure of it. And he needed to do the right thing, but…marry Fern? Could the solution really be that simple? And that…exciting?

He was just about to the door when he glanced to the right, into the little library. There was Fern, talking to the veteran Bob Eakin with animation, a book in her hand.

He could sneak past her and leave. Or he could do the right thing.

She'd probably be glad if he didn't stop in. She wouldn't want to see him before their pre-arranged time. If then. She had no interest in seeing him anytime, really.

So he should go.

Instead, he turned and walked into the library.

Bob gave him a knowing look. "I'd better get down to the cafeteria if I want to hold my table," he said, winking at Carlo as he headed out the door. "That Minnie Falcon is always trying to steal my window seat."

"But... Oh." Fern watched the old man's surprisingly rapid exit and then looked at Carlo without the faintest hint of happiness. More like resignation. "What are you doing here?"

"Visiting my grandpa. And Miss Minnie Falcon." He looked around to make sure no one else was in the room, then closed the little library's door. "Fern, we need to talk, and soon. Rumors are spreading."

Her lips tightened. "I said I'd meet you for dinner. Tomorrow."

"I'm worried it's not soon enough. Where's Mercedes?"

"She's at her day care program. I wanted to keep her in her routine, so she's still going part days even though I'm on vacation." She sounded defensive.

"Good," he said. "Would you want to go have lunch and talk about it now? Because I'm worried she'll hear something soon."

Fern looked at him and he read the struggle on her face. "I have to finish up here," she said. "I handpick books for a few of the residents."

"That's fine, I can wait. Or I can read. Or I can help."

"Fine," she said, stress evident in her voice. "Wait here." She turned on her heel and spun out of the library.

Leaving Carlo to stare down unseeingly at the stack of books in front of him and wonder just what he was going to propose during the lunch to come.

Chapter Twelve

An hour later, Fern sat across from Carlo at the back of the Chatterbox Café, feeling incredibly awkward.

Why was he treating her so gently, as if she was about to shatter? Did he think she wasn't strong enough to face the truth of the situation, the fact that she might very well lose Mercedes?

Well, he might have a point. She *wasn't* strong enough for that.

The café was bustling, full of moms with children, the police chief and one of the officers, some workmen from down at the pretzel factory. Waitresses in pink shirts rushed around with trays and pots of coffee. Through the large windows at the front of the restaurant, Rescue River's main street was visible, picturesque with snow.

Fern could smell burgers and fries, which she normally loved. Now the greasy odor turned her stomach. She grabbed a plastic-coated menu from the stand on the table and stared at it, barely seeing it.

But it beat staring at Carlo, who was even more handsome now that he was clean shaven. He'd hung up their winter coats, and his short sleeves revealed his massive soldier arms. Without the beard stubble, his jaw looked even more square, and his eyes, as he watched her, shone dark blue and honest.

She had to keep reminding herself that he'd misled her and Mercedes, not letting them know his beliefs about being Mercedes's father.

She pinched the back of her hand, hard, to distract herself from the emotional pain of Carlo's betrayal and of losing Mercedes.

"Thank you for coming," Carlo said, still sounding cautious.

"Sure. We have to talk. It's just…hard."

"I know, and I'm sorry. How do you think we should tell her?"

She shook her head. "I'm worried she'll be upset. Especially if she thinks there's going to be a change in her living situation. Which… there will be." Her stomach lurched as she said the words, and her eyes filled with tears.

"Um, about that." Carlo reached across the

table and took her hand. "I have an idea." He ran his thumb over her knuckles in a back-and-forth motion.

Even that light touch took her breath away. She tugged her hand back. "What's your idea?"

He took a deep breath and then blew it out. "This is going to sound crazy, but…we could get married."

Fern's heartbeat accelerated as everything around them seemed to fade away.

Marriage. To Carlo. A real family. Fun and caring and sweet, sweet togetherness. Her heart seemed to expand in her chest.

When she didn't answer, he continued talking. "I don't mean a regular marriage. I wouldn't expect that. It would be for Mercy's sake."

She stared at him. His mouth kept moving, but she'd stopped processing the words.

She'd gotten stuck on two particular phrases.

We could get married, which had made her heart soar.

I don't mean a regular marriage, which had brought her right back down to earth with a crashing thud. Of course someone like Carlo wouldn't be able to really love someone like her.

"Can I take your order?" came a perky voice. It was Lindy Thompson, who'd just graduated from high school last spring. She was a sweet and pretty girl, and Fern liked her because she was a reader who made regular appearances in the library.

"Hey," Lindy said, staring at Carlo. "You're that big war hero, right?"

A flush of color crossed Carlo's face. "I'm a veteran, but no big hero."

"No, I remember hearing about you in town. I was telling my brother he should meet you. Didn't you get a whole bunch of medals?"

He rubbed the back of his neck. "I may have a few. Who's your brother? Is he a vet, too?"

"Yeah, and he's not doing so well." Lindy's mouth turned downward. "He's got to go have some more surgeries just as soon as he's up for it, but we don't know when that will be."

"I'm sorry. You give him my best, will you?"

"Oh, thank you, I will! That's really nice of you!"

Okay, enough. The girl's eyes held the kind of hero worship that was pretty much irresistible to men. Great.

"Hey, maybe you could meet him sometime," Lindy suggested. "It would mean a lot to him. Sometimes he and Mom come in for lunch."

"Sure," Carlo said easily. "I'm in town for a while."

Lindy took their orders and Fern struggled with an absurd sense of jealousy.

Carlo didn't really want to marry her. Much more suited to him would be someone like pretty, young, outgoing Lindy. Just look at him, how handsome he was, how modest about his war achievements, how kind to a young waitress. He was a catch, all right, and in a little town like Rescue River, he'd be snatched up immediately. By someone much more fun and lively than Fern.

"So," Carlo said after Lindy walked away, "guess my suggestion fell flat."

She bit her lip. *No, it sounded wonderful!*

"I mean that we should get married."

This was the moment. She could agree to a marriage and have the wonderful family feeling she'd tasted during the storm.

Only it wouldn't be real.

"It would never work," Fern said. Better to pull the Band-Aid off quickly.

He swallowed visibly, opened his mouth as if to argue, and then closed it again. "Then, we should tell her together."

Fern forced herself to shrug and nod. "Sure."

"That way," he said, "she'll be more comfortable. So she can ask questions."

Push him away, push him away. "She'll have a lot of them. Not only about why you weren't there for her first four years, but about why you didn't tell us the truth during the snowstorm."

Carlo closed his eyes for a second and then reached out and took her hand, his expression regretful. "I want to build a relationship with you and I know it got started wrong."

The feel of his hard, large, calloused hand seemed to burn her. Her heart raced and she snatched her hand back, feeling heat rise in her face. "There's no relationship."

"Why?" He sounded bewildered. "Fern, I know I was wrong not to tell you my suspicions, but you of all people ought to know what it's like. We were practically strangers. I didn't know how to bring it up, or if I should. Things got away from me, but I never intended to deceive you."

She drew in a breath between clenched teeth. "Stop it."

"Stop what?"

"Stop acting so nice." Fern's throat closed up, and tears burned her eyes.

Don't you dare cry. The words of one of her particularly harsh foster mothers echoed in her mind. She'd learned to hold back her feelings then, and she could still do it. Again she pinched the back of her hand, hard.

Carlo leaned closer. "Fern. I want to work this out."

"It's not going to work out. How can it? You're her father, and you have the right to her. She likes you. It'll be fine for her. I'll just be a memory in her life, someone who took care of her for a little while until her daddy could come." Her voice squeaked and she clenched her mouth shut. Enough talking.

"Fern. I'm drawn to you. Are you sure you won't consider—"

"No!" He wanted a marriage of convenience, not of love. He didn't care for her as a woman.

"Why?" He was looking at her steadily. "Maybe there's a way we can work together. We certainly have to work together to tell Mercedes."

If she agreed to it, she'd be making a mockery of something that was supposed to be sacred. And she'd die a little more every day, living with Carlo and knowing he didn't love her.

She hardened herself to the hurt and concern on his face. "Didn't anyone ever tell you that no means no?"

He gave her a long, pained look and then broke eye contact and slumped back in his chair, seeming to shrink before her eyes.

Lindy approached with their food and Fern used the brief interruption to take deep, calming breaths. She could get through this. For

Mercedes's sake, she had to. Had to hand the child off graciously to him, could never let Mercedes suspect that her daddy had broken Mama Fern's heart.

The bells on the front door jingled, and Lindy put their plates in front of them and looked toward the restaurant's entrance. "Hey, it's my mom and brother. If he's feeling okay, can I bring him over for a minute?"

"Of course." Carlo's voice sounded stiff and formal.

"Mom," Lindy called. "Over here."

A tired-looking fiftysomething woman, whom Fern had also seen at the library, was struggling to get a wheelchair through the door. In it was a man who couldn't be more than twenty-one. He wore a hoodie and flannel sweats, and his head rested in a special support.

A couple of men near the front hurried to help with the door, and the older woman looked up, saw Lindy beckoning and headed over, a wide smile creasing her face.

"Mr. Camden, sir, I'd like you to meet my brother. Tom," Lindy said to the man in the wheelchair, "this is the one I told you about, who became a missionary? The Purple Heart, Silver Star guy? Say hi."

The man in the wheelchair didn't seem to

be able to move much, but he lifted his eyes to meet Carlo's.

Carlo was out of the booth in a flash, squatting to put himself on the same level as the man in the chair. "My pleasure," he said. Then he lifted his hand in a slow salute. "Thank you for your service."

The man in the chair blinked and swallowed and gave a little nod, and Lindy reached out to put an arm around her mom, whose eyes were shiny.

In the space of a few seconds, the two men seemed to exchange some knowledge that none of the rest of them could share.

"Would you like to join us?" Carlo asked, still kneeling.

The man shook his head, making garbled speaking sounds. He looked up at his mother and tapped his chest.

"He wants me to show you his medals," she interpreted, and reached into a bag attached to the wheelchair. She pulled out a small box and flipped it open. "He got the Purple Heart. We carry 'em all the time."

Fern watched, her food forgotten, as Carlo looked at the medal and then talked with the family about the younger man's combat. He was obviously comfortable with the man's disability and with the family as he walked with them to another table in the diner.

All Fern could think was what a good daddy he would be for Mercedes. And how proud and happy the woman would be who won his love.

He came back in and sat down across from her, looked ruefully at his cold burger and her untouched chicken salad. "I'm sorry about that," he said, still sounding polite and distant.

"It's fine. When…when do you want to meet with Mercedes?" His kindness and heroism just made it harder to think of how he'd probably take Mercedes and go somewhere else. Now she just wanted to get out of the café before she fell more in love with him. More impossibly in love.

"Well," he said, looking down at the table, "given the fact that Gramps already knows, and he didn't hear it from me, I think we should move fast. How about tonight?"

She didn't think she could bear another encounter with Carlo in one day. But she also wanted to protect Mercedes, and after the emotional encounter they'd just had with the wounded veteran, talk about Carlo would be all over town. "Okay," she said, "where?"

"Where does she feel most comfortable? Would that be out at the rescue, since you're staying there, or would it be at your home?"

Fern drew in a deep breath. The last thing she wanted was to have her cozy little retreat invaded by giant, gorgeous Carlo. Once he'd been there, she might never be able to exorcise the memory of him.

But that was the place where Mercedes felt at home, and Mercedes's needs took precedence. In fact, Fern had promised her that they could spend some time at home, among her familiar toys and games, tonight.

"All right," she said with a sense of impending doom. "Why don't you come over after dinner tonight?"

That evening, Carlo approached Fern's little bungalow as the sun sank below the trees that lined the snowy street. The house was in a neighborhood, but separated from the other houses by a little more land and a row of pines. That was perfect for Fern; she'd want to be able to keep to herself, but she was an integral part of the community, as well. In her quiet way, she helped others, from the kids at the library to the shut-ins at the Senior Towers. She might not know it, but everyone loved her.

He was in a fair way to falling in love with her himself. Which was bad, because she'd given him a definitive no today at lunch. And as she'd pointed out, no meant no. His face heated at the memory.

Seeing lights inside, he tapped lightly on the door, but no one came to open it. He pounded louder and rang the doorbell.

"Sorry," Fern said as she opened the door, her voice breathless.

"We were making a cake!" Mercedes added, popping out from behind Fern. "'Cause Mama says there's a surprise!"

"There *is* a surprise," he agreed, smiling at Mercedes, his heart pounding. How would she react when she learned he was her father?

He'd called Daisy for advice and strategies about how to talk to Mercedes, and she'd offered to call Fern as well, so that they were on the same page. They had to tell her together, reassure her that she was loved, let her know the progression and what would come next.

What *would* come next? Carlo didn't know. He wanted to have Mercedes, to raise her. More and more, he thought he'd like to do it in the little town of Rescue River, where she was already comfortable, where she had friends and a day care and a church home, where she'd have an aunt and a great-grandpa who loved her.

"She'll surely transition to living full-time with you," Daisy had said, "provided all the tests come back positive. But don't promise that. Let her know that the judge will decide what's best for her."

The whole situation had his heart aching and his stomach in a knot. This little girl had already faced so much loss, and he hated the idea of taking her from her very special Mama Fern.

On the other hand, he wanted to know her and love her and raise her. And it didn't look as though Fern would be able to get along with him to do that. He'd screwed up, plain and simple. He should have been easy and honest and up-front, and things might have been different.

But for better or worse—in this case, for worse—he wasn't a trusting guy who could spill his guts at a moment's notice, express a thought as soon as he had it. In that, as in so many things, he and Fern were alike.

"Come on, come see my house!"

He slid out of his snowy boots, catching a whiff of chocolate as he let Mercedes pull him through the little cottage in his sock feet. He got a quick impression of a cozy gas fire, polished wooden floors with colorful throw rugs, and books. Lots and lots of children's books, on shelves and stacked on end tables and in a basket beside Mercedes's booster chair in the dining room. Among the stuffed animals piled in an armchair, he recognized Peter Rabbit and Paddington and the Stinky Cheese Man, who'd made Mercedes laugh hysterically each night during the snowstorm. And there was a Madeline doll; he recognized the character from childhood reading with Angelica.

On a whim, he picked up the doll and made her recite a couple of lines from the Madeline book to Mercedes, and was rewarded when Fern and Mercedes recited the next line back at him.

"Come see the cake!" Mercedes shouted impatiently, tugging at him.

"You keep on surprising me," Fern said, smiling up at him. "Did you read that book to your sister?"

"At least five hundred times." He swallowed, tried to steel himself to the effect of her innocent smile. "Has Angelica seen this place? She'd love it."

Fern nodded. "She and Xavier have been over here a few times."

Carlo pondered that as Mercedes showed him around the little downstairs. So Angelica and Xavier had been here, not knowing that they were actually related to Mercedes.

The deceit just went on and on. Kath had never wanted to meet his family, and she'd stayed away from Rescue River during their short and stormy marriage, but what had brought her here in the end? He might never know.

"Come see my room and my kitty cat!" Mercedes ordered.

"Okay with you?" he asked Fern.

"Sure."

Mercedes took them both by the hand and pulled them up half a flight of stairs and into a bedroom so sweet and girlie that it took Carlo's breath away.

What he wouldn't have given to be able to provide Angelica with such a room back when they were kids. All pink and ruffly, with books on the shelves and a cozy window seat. More stuffed animals on the bed and a small table with a plastic tea set on it.

He was beyond thrilled that Mercedes had such a wonderful place to live. How could he take it away from her? How could he possibly compete?

Mercedes jumped up and down on her bed. "When you turn the lights off, there's stars!" she said. "Do it, do it, Mama!"

"When you stop jumping on the bed," Fern said, looking stern.

Mercedes clapped her hand to her mouth. "I forgot." She sat down properly on the bed, hands folded.

"Okay, ready?" Fern asked.

"Ready," Mercedes said.

Carlo found his throat just a little too tight to speak.

Fern turned off the light and the ceiling glowed with stars. Through the window, the purple and pink and orange shades of sunset showed above the evergreen trees.

"Mama Fern wanted to make my room fancy and special, like me," Mercedes explained reverently.

Wow.

After a minute, Fern flipped on the lights. "Cake next, or do you want to show Cheshire?"

"Cheshire!" Mercedes cried.

"He's probably hiding in my room," Fern said. "Why don't you go pick him up, very carefully, and bring him in here?"

"Mr. Carlo could come see your room."

Both adults shook their heads immediately. Though Carlo wouldn't have minded seeing what kind of bedroom Fern had created for herself.

After he'd met the cat, who looked decidedly unhappy to be awoken from his nap and manhandled by an overenthusiastic four-year-old, they headed down the stairs, Mercedes running ahead.

He touched Fern's arm, stopping her. "You've

made a wonderful life for her here, Fern, and I appreciate that more than you'll ever know."

She met his eyes, the muscles in her throat working, and didn't say anything.

"Look, I decorated it myself!" Mercedes cried from the kitchen.

Carlo followed Mercedes into the eat-in kitchen complete with old white appliances and blue-and-yellow curtains at the windows. On the counter was a lumpy-looking chocolate cake, decorated with an overabundance of sprinkles and M&M'S candies.

Fern took a deep breath. "Let's sit around the table and have dessert," she said, her voice just a little shaky, "and then we'll have our talk."

Carlo poured milk while Fern cut cake and Mercedes set out napkins and forks, and just like during the snowstorm, he got a feeling of family. And he liked it. A lot.

If only…

Fern cleared her throat. "So," she said, pushing cake around on her plate, "Mr. Carlo and I have something to tell you."

"When's the surprise?" Mercedes asked, her mouth full. "Is it after the talking? Did you bring it with you?"

"Oh, honey," Fern said with a laugh that sounded forced, "the surprise isn't a present. It's…news."

Mercedes cocked her head to one side and looked from Fern to Carlo. "Okay." Her voice was a little subdued, and Carlo couldn't tell if that was because she wasn't getting a present or because she sensed something momentous.

No point in delay. His heart felt as if it was going to pound right out of his chest. "The news is," he said, "that I'm your daddy."

The child's eyes widened with delight. "I got a daddy? Like Xavier?"

"No," Fern said in a controlled voice, "he's your daddy because once, a long time ago, he was married to your mommy."

Mercedes looked puzzled. "But Mommy went to heaven."

"That's right, and your daddy was far away and didn't know."

She patted his arm, looking concerned. "Were you sad? Because it's okay to be sad."

"Yes," he said truthfully. "I was sad. But when I got here, I found out something very happy. I found out about you!"

Mercedes studied him for a minute as though she was thinking hard. "You could stay with me in my room," she said, "but I think mommies and daddies are s'posed to sleep in one bed."

"Oh, no," Fern corrected, a pretty flush crossing her face. "Mr. Carlo isn't going to be that kind of daddy. He's going to live some-where else. Like…like Bryson's dad."

"And you can have a room there, too," Carlo hastened to add, wondering if Fern or Angel-ica would help him decorate it, since his skills were minimal in that department.

Mercedes's lips pursed out in a pout. "I want the kind of daddy who lives in the same house."

Fern reached over to give her a side hug. "Things can't always be just the way we want them to be, Mercy," she said in a low voice.

Mercedes struggled away and stood up, hands on hips, cake smeared across her face. "Wait. Mama Fern's still gonna 'dopt me, right?"

Fern looked at Carlo and he looked back at her. This was the tricky part. What had Daisy advised? He tried to remember the words he'd practiced.

Fern spoke up. "Since you have a daddy now," she said carefully, "you might not need to be adopted."

Mercedes's eyes went huge and she climbed into Fern's lap. "I wanna be 'dopted!"

Fern's arms went around Mercedes and she didn't look at Carlo. "I'll still see you lots and lots, I hope."

"We both love you," Carlo chimed in, his heart aching. "That doesn't ever go away or stop."

"Where am I gonna sleep?" Mercedes asked, her voice rising. "I get scared in the dark. I can't go to sleep without Mama Fern."

"I know." Fern's voice was broken. "It's hard."

Mercedes clung to Fern then, burying her head in Fern's shoulder, crying. Gone was the happy, confident little girl who'd led him all around her house. Carlo sat helpless, staring at the misery he'd caused.

"I don't wanna go with him," Mercedes said through her tears, looking up at Fern.

"Shh," Fern murmured, rocking her a little. "Shh, it's okay. You're staying with me for now. For a little while."

"You said it was a surprise, but this isn't a good surprise."

Fern grabbed a tissue and wiped her eyes and nose, took a gulp of milk. A deep, audible breath. "It *is* a good surprise, even if you feel a little sad now. It's wonderful to have a daddy. Daddies are lots of fun."

"But I want *you*, Mama Fern. I need a mommy!" She paused, rubbing her hand across her nose. "I'm sorry I jumped on the bed. I won't do it anymore."

"Oh, honey." Fern's arms tightened around

the little girl. "It's not your fault. You're a wonderful girl."

"Then, why can't I get 'dopted and stay with you?"

"We'll keep talking about it," Fern said. "We'll get to talk to a judge who will help us figure it all out."

"I don't wanna." Mercedes peeked out at Carlo then, her face thunderous. "You go away, mean man."

"Mercedes!" Fern drew in an audible breath. "We use nice words and respect."

Carlo waved his hand. "It's okay. Maybe it's best that I go for now?" He had no idea how to fix this.

He should never have come home. He should have stayed away.

"It might be best," Fern agreed with a slight catch in her voice. "We'll get together with you again…real soon. Maybe meet with Daisy."

"Okay," he agreed, and escaped out the door.

Chapter Thirteen

"Thanks for picking me up," Fern said to Susan Hayashi on a cold Saturday morning. The past couple of weeks had been awful, and she'd wanted to beg off from the church ice-skating outing and hole up at home. But the fresh air would be good for Mercedes. And the companionship, because Susan was bringing Roxy, one of the kindergarten-age kids she tutored.

They moved Mercedes's car seat into Susan's little car, and Susan cranked up a CD of kids' music, adjusting the sound to be louder in the back. As they headed down a country road, Fern heard Mercedes laugh in the backseat. She sighed with relief.

"Rough day?" Susan asked.

"Rough two weeks." Since Mercedes learned about Carlo being her father, a reality that the paternity test had confirmed, she'd had tantrums almost every day, along with bed-wetting and nightmares most nights. Mercedes wasn't getting much sleep, which meant that Fern wasn't, either. The strain was showing on both of them.

"Is it about Carlo?" Susan asked quietly. "I don't mean to be nosy, but the news is all over town that he's Mercedes's dad."

"Yep, that's what it is." Fern didn't exactly want to talk about it, but on the other hand, she had to talk to someone. "This is just between us, okay?"

"Sure."

Fern cocked an ear back to make sure the girls were doing okay. When she turned around, she was glad to see them bent together over Roxy's handheld game as the preschool music blared.

"She won't go with him," Fern said quietly to Susan. "He's supposed to have visits every other day, to get her used to the idea of him being her father and to prepare for her possibly living with him. But she hides in her room or has a huge tantrum. If he takes her, I hear her screaming all the way down the street."

It was awful, wrenching. Carlo had rented an apartment just a couple of blocks away from her house, and he'd bought toys and games and tried to make the place comfortable for his child, but she was having none of it.

"Is she afraid of him?" Susan asked. "I mean, he's kind of…large."

"I don't think it's that. He's so gentle with her. I think it's that she sees him as taking her away from me."

"Which he's doing," Susan observed.

"Well, maybe. The hearing might be as soon as next week, and then we'll know for sure how it's all supposed to turn out. But meanwhile, they need to spend time together."

"Is she clinging to you?"

Fern nodded. "Either that, or defying and hitting me. It's crazy."

Susan turned onto a smaller, snow-packed road, handling the car skillfully as it slid a bit. "It's actually pretty normal."

"Really?"

The young teacher nodded. "From all my coursework in special ed, I know that kids lash out at caregivers a lot when they're making a transition. On some level, they feel as though the parent they're attached to is pushing them out."

"That makes sense." She looked out the window at the wintry farmscape, remembering her own multiple transitions between homes. She'd never struck a foster parent, but there had been plenty of times she'd just given up and withdrawn. "I was in foster care myself, so I feel for her," she said to Susan, surprising herself. Mostly, she kept the details of her childhood private, but Susan's accepting friendship made her comfortable, as though she could let down her guard.

"Really?" Susan glanced over at her, eyebrows raised. "That must have been hard. Is Mercedes's situation bringing up all that for you?"

Fern cocked her head as she thought about it. "You're really smart, you know? I've been feeling incredibly blue and awful, and it's mostly about losing her, but it's…it's weird. It feels as if it's me getting abandoned and pushed out, a kind of hole inside I haven't felt in a lot of years."

"Childhood can come back to haunt you like that," Susan said in a tone that suggested she had a few childhood issues of her own to deal with.

As they pulled up to the lake—more of a small pond, really, with lots of children and adults laughing and playing—Fern put a hand on Susan's arm. "Thank you again for getting us out," she said. "I really want Mercedes to have a good time and just be a child. Stuff like this is perfect."

"Stick with me, kid." Susan smiled at her. "Seriously, you should hang out more with Daisy and me. We're the single supernerd girls of Rescue River, and we always have a good time."

"You're friends with Daisy?" Fern's stomach twisted. "My social worker? Are you going to tell her what we talked about?"

"You didn't say anything bad. But cone of silence anyway." Susan gave her a quick side-arm hug.

The girls started clamoring to join the fun, and Susan and Fern climbed out, too, to help them. "Daisy's great," Susan said. "You'll see, once she's not your caseworker anymore."

Yeah, great. That'll be when I don't have a kid anymore. Fern bit back a sigh. There was no reason she was entitled to have a child, just because she'd befriended Kath. It had been an unexpected gift and an honor that Kath had chosen her to raise Mercedes when she'd realized that she was terminally ill.

Fern had been in almost daily contact with Daisy since the blowup when Mercedes had found out Carlo was her daddy. Daisy had coached her about how to handle Mercedes's emotional storms, and had recommended consistent routines, an extra bedtime story and plenty of attention. According to Daisy, Fern was doing great. And Carlo, while he was visibly upset about Mercedes's rejection, wasn't taking it personally. He understood that a new change so soon after Kath's death was bound to upset Mercedes.

The thing was, though, that Mercedes needed closure. And so did she. Seeing Carlo almost every day wasn't helping her to care less for him. It just made her admire him more. His strength, his gentle patience, his efforts to make Mercedes laugh… It said a lot about the kind of man he was. He was a rock in the midst of a stormy time, and the temptation to cling to him grew bigger every day.

But she couldn't cling to a man who would never really love her.

Keep busy. She'd been following that mantra, working on her writing and illustrating when Mercedes was at Carlo's, putting in extra hours at the library.

Keep busy. Even now she needed to focus on the activity at hand, not go off into her own spinning thoughts.

She laced up her borrowed skates and followed Susan's lead, teaching Mercedes first to take giant steps in the skates on the nonslippery snow, and then heading out onto the pond for some very clumsy skating. Fern was learn-

ing right along with Mercedes, and she tried
to model good sportsmanship about her own
ridiculous lack of skill.

Finally, they got to where they could skate
slowly around the pond, holding hands, with
only a few falls. Thankfully, Susan had thought
of knee pads for the kids. Fern could have used
a pair herself.

Treasure each moment. It wouldn't be much
longer that she'd have this precious hand in
hers.

Afternoon sun peeked through the clouds,
casting a golden light on the pond, glinting off
the snow. She could smell the bonfire the guys
were already building in anticipation of staying through twilight. She didn't know if they
would stay; Mercedes's eyelids looked heavy,
a reminder that this was her nap time.

They needed to stick with regular routines,
as Daisy had been emphasizing. But then
again, it was important for them to have some
fun time together, to get out with other families and be social.

No matter how short or long was the time
she'd parent Mercedes, Fern knew she'd never
feel absolutely certain she was doing it right.
Parenting was complicated, requiring a million

little decisions. She had a renewed respect for all the parents she knew.

And doing it alone was more than challenging.

Fern thought of the time she'd spent with Carlo and Mercedes out at the farm. Thought of the happy moments at her house before the revelation that had shattered Mercedes.

Oh, she wanted that. She'd never known it before Carlo, but she wanted the whole lock, stock and barrel of family. Not just kids and pets, but a man.

Not just a man, but Carlo.

Throughout these past awful weeks, he'd never lost his temper, never yelled, never criticized. Compared to all the foster dads of her youth, he stood out as first-rate. Let alone that he was heroic, and handsome…and that he'd kissed her. For some time, however brief, he'd found her attractive.

It was enough to sweep a shy librarian right off her feet.

Beside her, Mercedes abruptly sat down on the ice—her preferred way of stopping—pulling Fern down, as well. Fern giggled and turned to the little girl. "What happened?"

But the question died on her lips. Mercedes was staring ahead, lower lip trembling, face flushing red. Meltdown warning signs.

Fern followed the little girl's gaze. Carlo.

Her heart thudded and she felt her breathing tighten.

Carlo skated slowly toward them and Mercedes scooted into Fern's lap. "I'm not going with him. Don't make me go, Mama. I'll be good."

Fern's heart constricted at the pain in the little girl's voice. It was pain she understood, but she also knew Mercedes had to get over it. "Tell you what," she suggested. "Let's show Mr. Carlo—I mean, Dad—how well you can skate."

"I don't want to show him. I wanna go home."

Fern struggled to her feet, but Mercedes's desperate clinging pulled her right back down again. "Don't make me go, Mama!"

Fern drew in a deep breath and fought for calm. People were staring, and if this was hard on her, it was twice as hard on Carlo and Mercedes. She closed her eyes and tried to pray, an effort that lasted only a couple of seconds before nerves made her open her eyes again.

"Hey, buttercup," Carlo said, coming closer and tweaking a lock of Mercedes's hair. "What's up?"

"Go 'way."

"She's doing a great job of skating," Fern said, meeting Carlo's eyes over the crying child. He was so handsome, and the pain and worry in his eyes made her ache for him.

"I wish she'd show me how to do it. I'm not very good."

Mercedes peeked out.

"Do you think if I just did it like this, it would work?" He leaned precariously out on one leg and fell.

Fern chuckled, knowing it took more skating skill to do what he'd done than it would to skate more normally. "Should we show him?"

"All right," Mercedes said reluctantly.

She got to her feet with Fern's help and together they took a few shaky, gliding strides across the ice. "See, Carlo," Fern called back, "you have to use two feet."

"Yeah," Mercedes added.

It was the most communication the child had offered Carlo since she'd learned he was her father. "Let's watch and see how he does," Fern suggested.

They turned and watched as Carlo glided on both skates, then lifted one leg out behind him and promptly fell.

"No, Daddy!"

She'd called him Daddy. Fern's world froze. From the looks of things, Carlo's did, as well.

"Do it like this!" Mercedes demonstrated.

"Do you want to hold his hand and show him?" Fern asked, her heart just about breaking. She pointed Mercedes toward her father, holding her lightly from behind.

"Would you?" Carlo held out a hand from his position, low down on the ice. "I think I need some help."

Fern watched, barely breathing, as the little girl slowly skated away from her to her father.

Letting out a sigh, Fern watched as Carlo carefully got to his feet and took Mercedes's hand.

The pair of them made a couple of rounds on the ice. Fern watched, her mitten pressed to her mouth, the other hand across her belly. What a bittersweet feeling. She didn't want to give up Mercedes, but she knew it was in the child's best interest to have a good relationship with her father. Which probably meant to live with her father. Not with her.

Problem was, she felt as if a hole had been cut in her gut.

She skated off by herself, looking out at the snowy fields. *Father God, I really need You here. I need to cling to You, because I have to learn how to let this little girl go.*

She didn't hear words for an answer, but from somewhere, calm crept over her. God was with her. God would make the outcome right. God would help all of them. Not that it wouldn't hurt, but the Lord would be there for her. She could lean on Him.

When Carlo brought Mercedes back, the little girl was full of pride. "I helped Daddy, Mama Fern! I helped him learn to skate!"

"That's great." Fern smiled and a painful peace, the Lord's peace, settled over her.

"Thanks, kiddo," Carlo said, patting Mercedes's shoulder as Roxy skated up.

"You're welcome, Daddy." She said it loud enough for her new friend to hear. Like Roxy, like most kids in Rescue River, she had a daddy now.

The two girls skated clumsily away, leaving Fern and Carlo alone.

"That went really well," she forced herself to say.

"Yes, I think she's opening up to me. She's precious. Amazing."

"She is." Standing here with Carlo, watching the child they both loved, felt like everything Fern had ever wanted.

"Are you sure we can't—"

He was going to talk about a pretend marriage again. And she couldn't trust herself to keep resisting, not with the way she felt about him. "No. We can't."

A muscle twitched in Carlo's square jaw as he looked away, back toward the crowd at the bonfire site. "Excuse me. I have to talk to someone."

"Okay." She watched him skate away, admiring his grace. Was there anything he didn't do well?

Would she ever stop feeling heartbroken over him?

And then she realized that Carlo was headed toward Daisy. Great. She watched as the two engaged in animated conversation. Carlo seemed to be trying to convince Daisy of something, because she shook her head, and he talked more, and then she cocked her head to one side as if she was considering.

What were they saying? Was he telling her how Mercedes had connected with him, meaning that now he could take Mercedes full-time?

Fern watched, her eyes blurring with tears, until Roxy bumped into her. "Sorry, Miss Fern!"

"It's okay." And then Fern did a double take. "Where's Mercedes?"

The girl shrugged. "She was crying. She didn't want to play."

Fern's Mom Radar turned on. "Where did you see her last, honey?" she asked as she scanned the pond.

"Over there." Roxy waved vaguely toward the wooded side of the pond and skated off.

Fern scanned the crowd at the pond. Pulled out her glasses, which she'd dumped because they kept fogging up, and scanned it again. Squinted to see the area the little girl had pointed out, now darkening in the late-afternoon gloom.

She started skating, searching frantically, a vise tightening around her chest. Where was Mercedes?

Carlo pulled his hood up against the increasing cold and nodded at Daisy. "I'm sure."

"Because if you change your mind," she said, "the judge could get irritable, think you're not stable. Which is the problem you face in your custody case anyway."

"Nope. Fern's her mother in every real sense of the word. I'm making arrangements for a better place to live, out in Troy and Angelica's bunkhouse, but that won't match what Fern has set up for her. I think we can work together and figure out a joint custody arrangement."

Daisy's face broke into a smile. "I love that you're looking at Mercedes's best interests. I'll start the paperwork tomorrow."

A frantic shout from the cluster of skaters in

the middle of the pond kicked Carlo's adrenaline on.

"Who's that yelling?" Daisy asked.

"Sounded like Fern." He turned and skated toward the crowd, heart racing. Fern wasn't a yeller, and that hadn't been a fun-loving shout. Something was wrong.

He reached her where she stood in the middle of the pond, face white. "It's Mercedes," she gasped out. "I've hunted everywhere and I can't find her."

Behind him, Daisy skated up while Susan came from the other direction.

"Let me check with Roxy," Susan said, pointing toward the child they'd come with, and skating over toward her.

"I already did," Fern called after her. "She said Mercedes was upset and wouldn't play. Oh, why didn't I keep closer watch on her?"

Carlo's pulse raced as he looked around the pond, trying to spot his daughter. "But she was so happy just a couple of minutes ago, skating with me."

"That's how she's been lately. Her moods have been really up and down." Fern was turning around slowly, shading her eyes, scanning the area. Her breath came in ragged gulps.

"That's normal with all she's been through." Daisy had a hand on his arm and another hand on Fern's. "Maybe she got overwhelmed with feelings. Some kids run off when that happens."

Carlo's heart was racing and his head spun with guilt. Had he caused this, somehow, by pushing Mercedes to skate with him? And it was cold out here, no place for a child to be alone as twilight fell. No telling who was lurking around, possibly meaning harm to a little girl. And the ice had been checked, but there was always the chance a fall or a current had made it thin.

But there was no time for emotions. And as Fern buried her face in mittened hands, her shoulders shaking, he realized he had to take the lead. Finding Mercedes was up to him.

"Everybody, gather round," he roared out in the same voice he'd used to command a company of soldiers. "Over here. Everybody. Now."

Members of their group skated their way quickly, seeming to recognize the seriousness in his voice.

Quickly he explained the situation to them, described what Mercedes was wearing. "Let's get organized. We need somebody to take care of the kids and keep them happy and together. And ask them what they saw without scaring them."

"I'll do that," Susan offered. "I know the kids."

"Keep them near the bonfire, and keep it stoked up," he said, making the plan as he spoke. "We'll need somewhere warm to bring her if we find her. *When* we find her." Important to keep everyone's confidence up. They *would* find her. They had to.

And they could use all the help they could get. "Someone needs to call the cops. I don't think there's anyone dangerous out here, anyone who could have taken her, but we should cover all our bases."

At that, Fern's sobs increased. He regretted having to say it, but there wasn't time to be sensitive, not now. If someone had taken Mercedes, every second was important.

"I'll call Dion," Daisy said, already on her phone.

People chimed in, offering to help, accepting his leadership without question.

He started assigning territory. "Ralph, right?" he said, pointing to a burly man whom he'd seen skating well. "You get a couple of people and cover this whole pond. Look for breaks in the ice, spots near the edge where a kid could hide or—" his voice cracked a little "—fall in. Here, punch your number into my phone first."

He turned to a woman who wasn't wearing skates, a sporty outdoors type who'd been helping to gather wood for the fire. "You get a group. Even numbers. Go through the woods in pairs. Stay where you can see each other."

She nodded, started pointing at people to help her, assigning them partnerships. Good.

"Parking lot," he said to the two remaining adults. "Look in and under every car. Give your phone numbers to Daisy and Susan."

Which left him and Fern, and she was shivering and sobbing. "Let's think," he said, putting an arm loosely around her. "There's no time for tears."

"But it was my fault!"

"Snap out of it!" He softened the words with a squeeze to her shoulders. "We know her best of all. You do. What kinds of places does she like to hide?"

"She likes to get into little places." She sniffed. "Like that book, *Hide and Seek Sammy.* Oh, Carlo, I'm so sorry."

"It's not your fault. Come on." He guided her over to the gathering area, found her a seat by the bonfire and sat down himself, removing his skates and pulling on his boots. "You stay here with Susan and Daisy and the kids. She'll be drawn to the fire as it gets dark, and I want you here." He gave Daisy a meaningful look. "I mean it, no searching. You stick together and wait for her."

Fern nodded, her shoulders still shaking. This highly competent woman had finally lost it.

"We'll find her," he promised. There was no room for doubt here, not in this type of situation. You had to keep your confidence up. "Pray. Hard."

He ran off toward the far side of the lake, checking every small spot, praying the whole time. *Lord, help me find her. Don't let me lose her before I've had the chance to be her dad. If You let me find her, I'll give her up, whatever she needs, whatever's right.*

He searched clumps of bushes, checked dry cattails sticking up through the ice. Waved and called encouragement to the other searchers. Went hoarse with calling his child's name.

His fingertips and his toes were going numb, and his face felt raw in the wind, but all he could think was how cold Mercedes must be.

He dipped in and out of the woods, because even though there were searchers there, he knew he was better trained than any of them. His eyes automatically scanned for small footprints and his ears were alert for little-kid cries.

But there was nothing. He'd gone most of the

way around the pond with no sign of her. His stomach tightened as he reluctantly concluded that someone might have taken her.

Please, Jesus, keep her safe.

Then he saw the outline of a rowboat, upside down, covered with snow.

In a flash he thought back to one of the stories they'd read together during the blizzard. Something about boats, all the uses of boats.

Upside down, it's a home for a clown. The picture had shown a clown peeking out from the edge of an upside-down rowboat.

Would she really?

He ran to the boat. The wind was fierce now, whistling through the pines, making his eyes tear up. He couldn't tell if the boat had been disturbed. "Mercedes?" he called, quieting his voice.

Was that a sound? Hard to hear over the wind, but maybe.

He heard it again as he lifted up the boat.

And saw a small, pink-and-purple-clad shape there. "Daddy?" the shape said with a little sob.

Thank You, Jesus.

He scooped her up in his arms, checked her limbs for injuries, kissed away her tears as she clung to him. "Are you okay? Do you hurt anywhere?" His heart was racing, now with joy, because she looked okay and she felt wonderful.

"I'm cold," she said, burrowing into his chest, crying. "I called and called but nobody came."

"Come on, let's take you to Mama." He shifted her to hold her even tighter against his chest, trying to warm her.

She nestled in. "I got scared," she said confidingly.

"Me, too, when I couldn't find you." Hugging her, he shot up another prayer of supreme gratitude.

Then, suddenly, she struggled violently to get out of his arms. He let her go, put her down on her skates but kept hold of her shoulders. "What's wrong, honey?" he asked, squatting down in front of her.

"Are you going to take me away now?" Her eyes were round, her voice worried.

After a moment's puzzlement, he suddenly understood her question and shook his head. "I'm not going to take you from Mama Fern," he said. "I'm going to take you back to her."

She hesitated, considering his words. "Really?"

"Really. Mama Fern needs you and you need her."

She held out her arms to him, and as he

picked her up and felt her arms go around his neck, a lump formed in his throat.

Holding her, looking around the darkening pond as it sparkled in the moonlight, he felt God's presence as never before in his life, and with it, a sense of calm came over him. God had it in control. God was making everything right, and He'd continue to do so.

Carlo couldn't even call out, he was so choked up, so he simply held Mercedes tight and set off at a fast walk toward the bonfire.

"Mama!" Mercedes cried when they got there, and Carlo put her into Fern's arms.

"You found her!" came Daisy's voice.

"Praise the Lord," Susan said as the kids cheered.

Fern didn't say one word, but her eyes, lifted to his, were filled with such gratitude and relief that he felt ten feet tall.

"Tell the others?" he asked Susan, whose eyes were wet.

"Of course." She headed off, calling in her strong voice.

"Oh, honey," Fern said, cradling Mercedes close, "are you okay? Let's get you right by the fire. Mama was so scared!"

"I did like the clown in the book," Mercedes said. "But it wasn't fun. And I was cold."

"Of course you were," Fern scolded, holding

Mercedes's small hands toward the fire, holding the child herself in her lap. She looked up at Carlo. "Thank you. Oh, Carlo, thank you so much. I'm so, so sorry I let her get lost."

He sat down behind them, wrapped both arms around them. "Thank God. Praise God."

Chapter Fourteen

A week later, as Fern parked in front of the dog rescue where she and Mercy had been stranded with Carlo, her mind played a movie of memories: hot chocolate and burned cookies, Carlo's deep rumbling laughter, his arm warm and protective around her shoulders. His tender kiss.

"My first sleepover!" Mercy bounced in her car seat. "Let's go, let's go!"

Mercy had clung to Fern for a couple of days after the near disaster at the skating pond, but then she'd gotten back into her four-year-old groove: playing hard at day care, eating and sleeping well at home, proving her resilience. And when she'd been invited to sleep over at Xavier's house for his birthday, she was over the moon.

Fern helped Mercy unhook her seat belt and then pulled the overnight case from the trunk.

"I'll carry my new sleeping bag," the child said, holding out her arms for the prized pink item.

Fern thought Mercedes was way too young for a sleepover, but Angelica, calling to invite her, had brushed aside Fern's objections. "She'll be fine here. She'll have Xavier, and her dad will be here, too. Her dad. I still can't believe Carlo has a daughter!"

So maybe it was okay. Fern's own childhood had been a little short on fun family sleepovers. What did she know about how to raise a child anyway?

Now Angelica opened the door, sank to her knees and pulled Mercy into a hug. "We're so glad you're here, honey! Come on in, it's cold out." She looked up at Fern. "Do you want to drop her off or stop in for a minute?"

Angelica's casual question surprised Fern. Was it normal to just drop off your four-year-old at someone's house?

"We have two other girls and three boys. It's going to get crazy, but I'll have plenty of help. I can handle it." Angelica got to her feet and held the door open, smiling at Fern.

"I'll come in," Fern said, "get her set up

and settled and make sure." She met Angelica's eyes. "I'm a little overprotective. I can't help it."

"Of course you are, after the scare you had."

"You heard about that. I feel awful that I let Mercedes get lost. It was all my fault."

"What, that she got lost?" Angelica's voice, which had sounded distracted and light until then, suddenly got focused. "Are you beating yourself up about that?"

"I should have been watching her every minute. I got upset and preoccupied and she was gone." She waited for Angelica's gasp of horror.

It didn't come. Instead, "Did I ever tell you about the time Xavier escaped from the hospital?"

"What? No."

"He got a whole block through downtown Boston. In a hospital gown, no less! And a complete stranger brought him back."

Fern leaned back against the doorjamb. "But that wasn't on your watch."

"Yes, it was. I had him out of his room in the playroom and got talking to one of the other moms. I looked up and he was gone."

"Wow." Fern took a deep breath and let it out in a sigh, some of her tension ebbing out with it. "I feel like such a bad mother."

"I know, right? But we're all bad mothers at times. Now come in and see what we're planning."

The living room where she and Carlo and Mercy had gotten to know each other was transformed with blue and green balloons and crepe-paper streamers. "Of course he wanted a puppy theme," Angelica explained. "Wait till you see the cake."

"It's shaped like a dog bone," Xavier shouted as he ran into the room, another boy racing behind him.

Quickly, Fern turned to check Mercedes's reaction. Would the older boys intimidate her?

But Xavier stopped in front of Mercedes, grabbed her hand and tugged her toward the kitchen. "C'mon, Mercy! We're cousins now, so you can come over all the time. But you're gonna have to learn to play fun games, not dolls."

"I play fun games." Mercy put a hand on her hip as if daring Xavier to disagree.

"Then, c'mon!"

The three kids ran off together without a backward glance.

"I'll, um, just put her stuff down, I guess." Fern set down the birthday present she and Mercedes had wrapped together, checked the overnight case again to make sure her daughter's favorite stuffed frog hadn't been forgotten.

"I'll take good care of her, don't worry. And Carlo will be here all night."

Fern's heart lurched. "Carlo's staying over?"

"Just for tonight, for the party. In fact, he should be here any minute. Troy and I can use the help, and we thought it would make Mercy more comfortable. I'm so excited to have a little girl in the family! I'm going to spoil her like mad."

Troy came up behind Angelica, smiling as he heard what his wife was saying. He put an arm around Angelica and patted her rounded belly. "Good practice for us."

"That's right," Angelica said, her dark eyes sparkling. "Pretty soon, Mercy will have a new baby cousin to play with."

"That's wonderful." Seeing the loving way the two of them looked at each other, Fern felt her heart aching. Maybe she and Carlo could have had something like that, if she hadn't blown it.

"In fact," Angelica said, "did Carlo tell you he's going to be moving into the bunkhouse as soon as the weather breaks? That way, Mercy can have room to run and play and get to know all of us better, and we can help when his new job starts up."

New job? "Great!" Fern tried to inject some excitement into her tone, but her stomach churned.

"You should take a look at the bunkhouse on your way out," Angelica encouraged. "I don't think it's locked. I fixed it up a little when Xavier and I were staying there, and it's really homey. Mercy will be super happy there."

Of course she would. "Okay, I will. Thanks."

Fern found Mercy and hugged her goodbye. "Daddy will be here. You go to him if you need anything."

"I will, Mama. I gotta go play." She struggled away and ran over to where Xavier and the other boy were dumping an army of plastic men on the floor.

Fern watched for another minute, then forced herself to walk out the front door. She waved to Angelica, who was greeting another mother and a pair of twin girls, and trudged toward her car.

"Leave her all day tomorrow if you want," Angelica called after her.

Fern waved back, unable to speak.

Mercy was fine without her. She was being embraced by Carlo's family. And what could Fern, a nerdy librarian, all alone in the world, offer Mercy that would compare with Carlo's wonderful family?

She drove a couple of hundred yards, but tears blurred her vision and she stopped to find a tissue. There was the bunkhouse. She blew her nose. Well, sure, she'd stop and take a look. It wasn't as if she had anything else to do.

She walked inside and looked around, immediately aware of how the pine-paneled walls, bright area rugs and colorful curtains said *home*. There were two small bedrooms and a kitchen along one side of the living area.

It was perfect for Carlo and Mercy.

A spasm of pain creased her stomach and she sank down into a rocking chair, wrapping her arms around herself for warmth, still in her winter coat.

She was going to lose Mercy.

Just as she'd already lost Carlo.

By ignoring his offer of a marriage of convenience, she'd given up all she'd ever wanted in life. Now that he saw what a bad mother she was, he'd never take her back. He'd never let her keep Mercy. What claim did she have on the child anyway?

And what claim did she have on Carlo?

She'd judged him and pushed him away. She'd been so harsh, refusing to accept his apologies even when he was so kind to her and Mercy. And then that horrible experience at the pond. Even now she remembered the terror she'd felt, thinking Mercy might have been drowned or kidnapped. And she remembered the sternness in Carlo's voice as he'd called everyone into action, worked to solve the problem, while Fern had fallen apart.

Now he was settling into the bosom of his family, and rightly so. He'd find another woman, someone who was outgoing and more motherly, someone who wouldn't let a child get lost, wouldn't pass judgment, wouldn't act shy.

And Fern would go on alone.

She'd lost it all.

She let her face sink into her hands, and in the despair of an aloneness she'd created for herself, she cried out to God.

"Isn't that Fern's car?" Troy said to Carlo an hour later. They were walking out to the kennels to get puppies for the kids to play with, having decided that Brownie and her pup needed to stay sequestered from the overenthusiastic kids.

Carlo glanced over, and just seeing her little subcompact stabbed him in the gut. "What's she doing at the bunkhouse?"

Troy shrugged. "You should go see."

Longing tugged at Carlo's heart, but he tamped it down and shook his head. "She doesn't want me anywhere around." He was trying to accept that no meant no, but it wasn't easy.

They walked to the kennel, where the silence between them was broken with loud barking. Troy grabbed a couple of leads and opened a kennel. "Leash up those two," he said, "and I'll get a couple more. We need sturdy pups for this crew."

As they brought the excited dogs to the house, Troy spoke up. "Seemed as if you and Fern had some feelings for each other. Might be worth a second try." He cleared his throat. "I'm not much on talking about my faith, but the second chance God gave me and Angelica has meant the world to me."

Carlo thought about that as he opened the front door and held it for Troy, laden down with a crate of three yipping pups. Could he open himself up to more rejection from Fern? And where was the line between hope and harassment, when she'd already given him a clear no?

"Daddy!" Mercy ran to him, hugged his leg and then squatted down to pet the dogs he'd brought in.

Troy met his eyes over the crate. "Might mean the world to her, too," he said quietly, nodding down at Mercy. "This back and forth from one house to the other can't be easy on her."

That was for sure. It wasn't easy on any of them. "I'll give that some thought," Carlo promised.

Fern didn't know how long she wrestled with herself, tears running down her face, praying for forgiveness.

Finally, the setting sun cast its rays through the bunkhouse windows, and she lifted her eyes to see God's glory painted across the sky in pink and purple and orange. At the same moment, she felt warmth and love embracing her.

Her heavenly father seemed to speak through the sunset, expressing His extravagant love for her. Forgiving her the faults that a childhood tainted by human sin had wrought in her. Offering the hope that she could learn, could grow, could love.

She wiped her eyes and let the forgiveness wash over her, soothing some of the heartache and loss.

A knock on the bunkhouse door had her blowing her nose and wiping her eyes again, running her hands over her hair.

"Fern! Are you in there? It's Daisy and Susan. We stopped in to wish Xavier a happy birthday and saw your car."

She drew a deep breath, waited for her usual antisocial desire to shoo away human contact.

But it didn't come. She actually wanted to see them. She hurried to the door and opened it.

"You've been crying!"

"What's wrong, honey?"

They wrapped her in hugs and worried questions, and soon all three of them were sitting at the bunkhouse's small dining table, drinking from juice boxes that were the only thing they'd found in the refrigerator.

"Did anyone check the expiration on these?" Susan asked, studying her box.

"They're full of preservatives. It's fine." Daisy waved a hand. "Fern. Are you going to tell us what's going on?"

"I'm just emotional about leaving Mercy overnight, that's all." Fern looked at her friends' skeptical faces and added, "Mostly."

Susan smiled sympathetically. "Get used to it. As a single mom, you've got to embrace time to yourself when you can find it. In fact, once you start dating, I'll gladly take a turn at babysitting."

"Me, too," Daisy said. "We're like the best babysitters in town."

"Because we love kids and I, for one, am never gonna have kids of my own."

"Me, either," Daisy said.

Susan nudged her. "Don't be too sure. With

the vibes I'm feeling between you and Dion, I'm thinking you might have yourself a white picket fence and a couple sweet little babies before you turn thirty."

"Susan!" Daisy's fair skin went pink. "That is *so* not happening."

Fern's memory conjured up the speedy way Daisy had contacted the handsome African-American police chief and how they'd shared a spontaneous hug when Carlo had come rushing across the frozen pond carrying Mercedes.

Daisy cleared her throat. "Change of subject. You heard that Carlo needs to adjust the schedule for Mercy's care, huh?" Her voice was businesslike as she switched into full social worker mode.

Fern could understand wanting to keep your personal life to yourself. "Yeah, only I don't quite understand what happened. When's the custody hearing?"

"Um, unless there's a problem, there's not going to be one."

Fern frowned at Daisy. "Why not?"

"Didn't he tell you he's not fighting for sole custody anymore? That he wants to do joint custody?"

"Nooo," Fern said as her world spun.

"You're kidding." Daisy stared at her, then

slapped her own forehead. "I'm so sorry, Fern. I should have told you, but I assumed that the two of you had talked it through. All we need to do is finalize the arrangements, figure out what days she's with you and what days she's with Carlo. In fact, I have papers for you to sign back at the office, if you're game."

Fern stared at the other woman, stunned. "You mean," she said faintly, "I can still be Mercedes's mom?"

"Yes! Yes! Oh, honey, I'm so sorry."

Fern buried her face in her hands, over-whelmed. Just like that, she was back to being Mercedes's mom. She had everything she'd hoped for. Only...

She felt a hand gently rubbing her shoulders from one side, and heard Daisy slide her chair over from the other. She looked up to see both women leaning toward her, concerned expressions on their faces.

"Are you okay?" Susan asked. "Isn't that what you wanted?"

She nodded quickly, blinking back tears. "I can't believe it. I can't believe I get to mother that wonderful child. Even after I screwed up so bad at skating."

Daisy patted her arm. "That could've happened to anyone. You're a wonderful mom,

Fern. You and Mercedes will be great for each other long-term. I'm so happy it turned out this way."

"Is it going to be weird," Susan asked, "working out joint custody with Carlo when you weren't even married to him?"

Fern nodded. "Yeah, especially when we're… basically not speaking to each other."

Susan gave her a hard look. "Does that bother you?"

"Well, of course it does." She opened her mouth to say something about communication being important for Mercedes's sake, but what came out was different. "I like him. A lot."

Susan lifted an eyebrow. "As in *like* like?"

"I'm not totally surprised," Daisy said. "You should let him know how you feel."

Fern heaved a sigh. "Easier said than done. He's just so *nice.* He'd do anything for Mercedes, but…I wish he liked me for me, you know?"

Daisy and Susan exchanged glances.

"It'll never happen," Fern said to forestall a pep talk. "I'm just not the type of woman men go for. And someone like Carlo, all handsome and hunky and kind? There's no way." As she said it, a heavy weight seemed to settle atop her heart.

Susan looked at Daisy. "Chatterbox?"

"It's two-for-one appetizers tonight," Daisy said.

"Come on, Fern," Susan said, reaching for Fern's hands and pulling her up out of her chair. "This calls for a lot more girl talk."

"Yeah," Daisy added, patting Fern's shoulder and then slipping into her coat. "Let's go get some dinner. It's five thirty and still a little bit light out. Spring's only a heartbeat away."

"The Chatterbox's fried zucchini will make everything better," Susan said.

But as she walked out of the bunkhouse with Susan on one side and Daisy on the other, Fern's heart ached.

She had Mercedes. She had friends. Life should be good.

But she didn't have Carlo. And wouldn't. Not ever. "I'm going to have to take a rain check, guys," she said.

Daisy eyed her sharply. "You going to be okay?"

Fern nodded. "I think…I just need a little time alone." And not just alone; she needed time with the Lord.

Carlo and Angelica were sitting at the kitchen table the next morning when a car door slammed outside.

Troy, spatula in hand, stepped from the stove to look out the window. "It's Fern," he said.

In the cool of the slightly drafty kitchen, Carlo started to sweat. He was about to do one of the hardest things he'd ever done in his life.

Fern knocked on the kitchen door and then opened it, sticking her head in. "Hey," she said with just a trace of librarian shyness.

Carlo's heart constricted at the sight of her. She looked stressed, as though she'd been crying. The fact that he'd caused more than some of that stress bit at him.

At least now he knew he was going to alleviate it.

Inside, she accepted hugs from Troy and Angelica and peppered them with questions about how Mercy had done and how they'd survived the party. She was coming out of her shell, and he knew without a doubt that every unattached guy in Rescue River would want her. What would it be like if she started seeing other guys? If she found someone special to be with, to help her raise Mercy?

The very thought made him nauseated.

"Sit down, I'll fix you some pancakes," Troy said. "You'll need your strength for the rest of the day. The kids didn't get much sleep last night."

"Aw, thanks, but I'm not hungry. Where are the kids anyway?"

"They're watching the end of a movie." Angelica lifted her hands in apology. "Sorry, I know you don't let Mercy watch much TV—"

"No problem! I totally understand." She turned to Carlo. "We need to talk," she said.

Dimly he wondered what she had to say to him, but whatever it was, it couldn't be as world changing as what he had to say to her. If she was going to tell him he was around too much, that he needed to back off, or that she'd decided to sue for full custody... Well, he could trump that.

Oblivious of the undercurrents, Troy flipped pancakes like a short-order cook. "So, Fern, what have you been up to?"

She shrugged, smiled at the man. "Actually, I've been writing and painting like crazy."

"That's so cool," Angelica said. "Our local librarian is going to be famous!"

She blushed and shook her head. "I doubt that, but it helps me to think."

"Did you hear about Carlo's new job?" Angelica asked. "Tell her, bro!"

Fern looked surprised and interested. "Where? Doing what?"

"A nonprofit that helps some of the migrant families," he said quickly, wanting to get the unimportant stuff over with. "They needed a Spanish speaker, someone with field experience in the country. I start next week." He looked over at his sister, his stomach churning. "Would you mind if we went for a little walk?"

"Go for it. Troy and I will finish cooking, and the kids are content here with the dogs." She gave him a tiny grin and a subtle thumbs-up.

Whatever that meant.

So they headed out the door and into the snowy countryside. The sky was a brilliant blue, and long icicles dripped from the eaves of the barn. In the distance, a farm truck chugged down the highway.

It was as good a time as any. "I've been thinking about something—"

"I've made a decision—" she said at the same time.

They both laughed, awkwardly. "You first," she said.

He swallowed. "Okay. Fern, I've gone over and over this situation with Mercy. I've thought about it and prayed about it and I can only think of one thing that's really best, best for both of you." He paused, his heart hurting, and then forced the words out. "You should take her full-time."

She'd opened her mouth to speak, but with

her words, her jaw dropped open and stayed that way a good few seconds.

He rushed on, wanting to get this over with. "It's not right to have a child go back and forth between two houses. She's happiest at your place, with her books and her cat and her stars on the ceiling. And with...with you, Fern. You're the best mother a little girl could ever hope for, and I trust you completely with her."

She was still staring at him.

Why wasn't she saying anything? "Of course, I'd hope you would let me have visitation rights. I want to be in her life," he said. "I mean, who am I kidding? I *want* to raise her. But for her sake—and for yours—I'll gladly give that up."

Silence. He couldn't interpret the look in her eyes. "What do you think?" he asked.

"Carlo." She took his hand in her smaller ones, staring up at him.

Being this close to the woman he loved made him a little dizzy. "Yeah?"

"You'll never believe this, but...I was going to offer the same thing. I've been up all night, reading my Bible and thinking about it, and I realized that Mercy would do fine being with you full-time."

"But—"

She stopped his protest with a finger to his

lips. The touch was quick and soft, like the feather of a bird, but it took his breath away.

She went on, her voice resolute. "You have a great family. I mean, look at all this." She waved a hand, encompassing Troy and Angelica's house and the rescue barn and the snowy fields around them. "But more than that, you're a great dad. And, well, it's time to think about what's best for her, not for me."

He couldn't believe what he was hearing. He cocked his head to one side. "You'd sacrifice what you want for me and Mercy?" he asked.

She nodded. "Once I got my head on straight, yeah, I would. It's the only thing to do. When you care about someone, you want the best for them."

"That's what I thought, too."

They were quiet for a minute, staring at each other. Around them, sunlight sparkled on snow.

A chilly wind loosened a lock of hair from Fern's red cap. He brushed it back with a finger, thinking he'd never seen anything so beautiful as her face. "What part of the Bible were you reading?"

She cocked her head to one side. "King Solomon?"

Of course. He nodded slowly. "It just doesn't seem right to divide the living child in two, not when she has a perfectly wonderful mother and home."

"What happens," she asked in a voice that was barely louder than a whisper, "if *both* parties want to keep the child whole?"

The question hung in the frosty air between them.

Her bare hands looked cold, so he encased them in his larger ones. "I asked you before if you would marry me," he said, "but you turned me down. Would you... Could you reconsider?"

When she shook her head decisively, his heart sank.

"No, Carlo," she said, squeezing his hand, her eyes going shiny. "No! I just can't. I can't pretend about something as important as marriage."

"I wouldn't be pretending," he blurted out.

Her eyebrows shot up into her hairline. "You wouldn't?"

He shook his head. "I think I fell for you the first night I saw you, taking such good care of a little girl I had no idea was mine, bringing me soup in a storm." He smiled a little, remembering. "That feeling's only grown over time, as I've gotten to know you. You had a bad start, Fern, just like I did, but you didn't let it stop you from loving and helping and being part of the community." He paused, unaccustomed to making such a long speech, but he felt as if his life and his future depended on it.

The occasion demanded something else, too. He sank to his knees in the snow. "The fact that you'd be willing to give Mercy up, for her own good... That just seals it, Fern. You're the woman I want to spend the rest of my life with. I know you said no before, but do you care at all about me? Maybe even enough to marry me?"

"For Mercy or for real?" she asked, her eyes wide and insecure.

"For real." He kissed her cold hands, each one, and then wrapped them together in his own larger ones. "Totally for real." He held his breath.

"Then...yes!" She sank down to her knees, facing him, as his heart soared. "Oh, Carlo!"

He clasped her to him and felt that everything he'd ever dreamed of was right there in his arms.

Moments later, she lifted her head. "Do you want to go tell Mercy?" she asked. "As her daddy, I think you should do the honors."

Carlo stood and pulled her to her feet. He tucked her under his arm and pressed her close to his side. "I think," he said, "we should do it together."

Epilogue

"I am so not a party person." Fern taped the end of the last crepe-paper decoration into place and surveyed it, frowning. It looked crooked.

"It's for a good cause," Carlo said as he dumped a load of firewood into the holder beside the fire.

She smiled at her husband, taking her time to enjoy the view of his muscular arms emerging from rolled-up flannel shirtsleeves. "Two good causes. And it's my favorite kind of party—small."

She looked around the room with satisfaction. They'd bought this little farmhouse only two months ago to accommodate their growing family, and it was absolutely gorgeous. Fern had brought all her favorite things from her little cottage, and they'd hustled to get the decorating done in time for the holidays.

Right at the edge of town, the place perfectly accommodated her need for both social and quiet time.

Mercedes called from the living room, "Sissy and me are gonna go build a snowman to meet everybody, 'kay?"

Fern met Carlo's eyes. "Could you help them?"

"I'd love to."

And it was true, Fern thought as she watched him usher the two little girls outside. Carlo was a natural father. To Mercedes, of course, but he was the one who'd heard about Paula in his new job reaching out to migrant groups.

Adoption. It came naturally to Fern anyway, with her background and with the way she'd come to love Mercedes. There were so many children who needed homes. And Paula was exactly Mercedes's age. They'd had her for six months, and of course there were issues, but the two girls were already inseparable.

Carlo helped Paula form a snowball and then roll it into a snowman. The little girl's dark eyes shone as she emulated Mercedes and stared up adoringly at Carlo.

Smiling, Fern hurried back into the kitchen to stir the tortilla soup she'd prepared for this double celebration—housewarming and adoption. It was comfort food for Paula. And then she returned to watch her family out the window, sketch pad in hand.

She'd gotten the go-ahead on a new picture book, and she'd deliberately chosen to work with snowy landscapes and with a family much like her own. Far from halting her creativity, being a wife and mother only added to it.

Time was an issue, but with Carlo's encouragement, she'd gone down to half-time at the library. That way, she had some time to paint while the girls were in school, and time to nurture them when school was over.

Pretty near perfect.

The gates to their front yard opened and Susan and Daisy came in. Angelica and Troy were right behind them, carrying presents, with Xavier running ahead to meet the girls. They'd also invited Lou Ann Miller, Gramps and Miss Minnie Falcon, but the older generation had a birthday party to attend at the Senior Towers and they were coming later.

Fern put down her sketch pad and went out onto the porch. Carlo came to stand beside her as the girls ran ahead to greet the new arrivals.

Fern looked up at her husband and shut her eyes for a two-second prayer of thanks. Carlo squeezed her shoulders and kissed the top of her head. "See, a party isn't so bad," he teased.

"Not when it's all the people you love." Fern

slid an arm around his waist, and together, they went to bring their friends and family into their new home.

* * * * *

Dear Reader,

Thank you for reading *His Secret Child*! This book is especially close to my heart because Fern—introverted, bookish and creative—is a lot like me. Not to mention that some of my very favorite people are librarians! Portraying Fern's struggles to connect with others was easy because I've sometimes had similar ones. I'm also very aware that quiet people need human connections and love every bit as much as do more outgoing types—and that they have a lot to offer the world.

God made such an amazing variety of people, and it's fun to explore that variety as I dream up my characters and stories. Please visit my website at www.leetobinmcclain.com for more information about my books. You can even download a story for free!

Wishing you peace,
Lee

LARGER-PRINT BOOKS!

GET 2 FREE LARGER-PRINT NOVELS PLUS 2 FREE MYSTERY GIFTS

Love Inspired® **SUSPENSE**

RIVETING INSPIRATIONAL ROMANCE

Larger-print novels are now available...

YES! Please send me 2 FREE LARGER-PRINT Love Inspired® Suspense novels and my 2 FREE mystery gifts (gifts are worth about $10). After receiving them, if I don't wish to receive any more books, I can return the shipping statement marked "cancel." If I don't cancel, I will receive 4 brand-new novels every month and be billed just $5.49 per book in the U.S. or $5.99 per book in Canada. That's a savings of at least 19% off the cover price. It's quite a bargain! Shipping and handling is just 50¢ per book in the U.S. and 75¢ per book in Canada.* I understand that accepting the 2 free books and gifts places me under no obligation to buy anything. I can always return a shipment and cancel at any time. Even if I never buy another book, the two free books and gifts are mine to keep forever.

110/310 IDN GH6P

Name	(PLEASE PRINT)

Address		Apt. #

City	State/Prov.	Zip/Postal Code

Signature (if under 18, a parent or guardian must sign)

Mail to the **Reader Service:**
IN U.S.A.: P.O. Box 1867, Buffalo, NY 14240-1867
IN CANADA: P.O. Box 609, Fort Erie, Ontario L2A 5X3

Are you a current subscriber to Love Inspired® Suspense books and want to receive the larger-print edition?
Call 1-800-873-8635 or visit www.ReaderService.com.

* Terms and prices subject to change without notice. Prices do not include applicable taxes. Sales tax applicable in N.Y. Canadian residents will be charged applicable taxes. Offer not valid in Quebec. This offer is limited to one order per household. Not valid for current subscribers to Love Inspired Suspense larger-print books. All orders subject to credit approval. Credit or debit balances in a customer's account(s) may be offset by any other outstanding balance owed by or to the customer. Please allow 4 to 6 weeks for delivery. Offer available while quantities last.

Your Privacy—The Reader Service is committed to protecting your privacy. Our Privacy Policy is available online at www.ReaderService.com or upon request from the Reader Service.

We make a portion of our mailing list available to reputable third parties that offer products we believe may interest you. If you prefer that we not exchange your name with third parties, or if you wish to clarify or modify your communication preferences, please visit us at www.ReaderService.com/consumerschoice or write to us at Reader Service Preference Service, P.O. Box 9062, Buffalo, NY 14240-9062. Include your complete name and address.

LISLP15

YES! Please send me **The Montana Mavericks Collection** in Larger Print. This collection begins with 3 FREE books and 2 FREE gifts (gifts valued at approx. $20.00 retail) in the first shipment, along with the other first 4 books from the collection! If I do not cancel, I will receive 8 monthly shipments until I have the entire 51-book Montana Mavericks collection. I will receive 2 or 3 FREE books in each shipment and I will pay just $4.99 US/ $5.89 CDN for each of the other four books in each shipment, plus $2.99 for shipping and handling per shipment.*If I decide to keep the entire collection, I'll have paid for only 32 books, because 19 books are FREE! I understand that accepting the 3 free books and gifts places me under no obligation to buy anything. I can always return a shipment and cancel at any time. My free books and gifts are mine to keep no matter what I decide.

263 HCN 2404   463 HCN 2404

Name	(PLEASE PRINT)	
Address		Apt. #
City	State/Prov.	Zip/Postal Code

Signature (if under 18, a parent or guardian must sign)

Mail to the **Reader Service:**
IN U.S.A.: P.O. Box 1867, Buffalo, NY 14240-1867
IN CANADA: P.O. Box 609, Fort Erie, Ontario L2A 5X3

* Terms and prices subject to change without notice. Prices do not include applicable taxes. Sales tax applicable in N.Y. Canadian residents will be charged applicable taxes. This offer is limited to one order per household. All orders subject to approval. Credit or debit balances in a customer's account(s) may be offset by any other outstanding balance owed by or to the customer. Please allow 4 to 6 weeks for delivery. Offer available while quantities last. Offer not available to Quebec residents.

Your Privacy—The Reader Service is committed to protecting your privacy. Our Privacy Policy is available online at www.ReaderService.com or upon request from the Reader Service.

We make a portion of our mailing list available to reputable third parties that offer products we believe may interest you. If you prefer that we not exchange your name with third parties, or if you wish to clarify or modify your communication preferences, please visit us at www.ReaderService.com/consumerchoice or write to us at Reader Service Preference Service, P.O. Box 9062, Buffalo, NY 14269. Include your complete name and address.

MMLPBPA15

READERSERVICE.COM

Manage your account online!

- Review your order history
- Manage your payments
- Update your address

> *We've designed the*
> *Reader Service website*
> *just for you.*

Enjoy all the features!

- Discover new series available to you, and read excerpts from any series.
- Respond to mailings and special monthly offers.
- Connect with favorite authors at the blog.
- Browse the Bonus Bucks catalog and online-only exculsives.
- Share your feedback.

Visit us at:

ReaderService.com

RS15